# WALSINGHAM'S PUPPETS

Book 3 in a 4 Book series, after the successful "Against All The Odds' and 'Tested To The Limit'

Lil Niven

Cover design by: Heather Niven

*This book is dedicated to my wonderful family - husband Pete, daughters Loraine, Elizabeth and Heather and grandson Aidan.*

# CHAPTER 1

There was great excitement at the manor of Sir Richard and Lady Joan Lovell on the day Francesca was to marry Lorenzo, her one and only love. The pair had found each other again after years of separation, brought about after Lorenzo had been accused of a murder he didn't commit. He had been forced to flee London in haste with just what he could carry and without an opportunity to explain his predicament to his fiancée. When Francesca repudiated the false charge against him and refused to forsake her love for him her father had disowned her and thrown her out into the street.

Lorenzo (or Luigi Guilliano as he was now known) had finally settled in Topsham, where he had opened a fencing school. Francesca, an excellent seamstress, had opened her own tiny shop in a small town about two hours ride from Topsham, under the name Caterina. Lorenzo knew she'd left London soon after him but had no idea of where she had gone or how to go about finding her. Unbeknown to him Richard had enlisted the help of Sir Francis Walsingham and his spy network to locate her and the search had been successful. Richard and Joan then arranged for the two to be reunited at their manor. Lorenzo and Francesca's love for each other proved to be as strong as it had ever been, and they were soon planning their long-postponed wedding.

Now that day was finally here. The wedding was to take place at the home of Richard's parents, Lord and Lady Lovell. Holyfield Hall previously belonged to Joan's father, Lord Thomas Marchemont, before he became involved in a treasonous plot. Upon discovery the Crown exiled him together with his treasonous son, Geoffrey, and seized his estate which Queen Elizabeth had then granted to Richard's father Edmund. Edmund had known Lorenzo since he had first arrived in Topsham and was pleased to offer his home and its private family church to him and Francesca for their wedding.

The bride travelled by coach from the manor where Richard and Joan lived to Holyfield Hall. Richard and Joan, who was now in the mid stages of her pregnancy, rode with Francesca in a coach bedecked with white roses and herbs which emitted a beautiful fragrance. The warm morning was bathed in unbroken sunshine, but a gentle breeze prevented the heat from becoming oppressive. A perfect day for a perfect wedding.

Francesca had made her own wedding dress with a little help from her newfound friend Joan.

She had crafted the forepart and sleeves from silk brocade the colour of newly unfurled beech leaves and the main body of the dress was made from satin of the darkest laurel green. The neck, the front of the bodice and the hem of the skirt had been adorned with exquisite needle lace from Flanders, a gift from Joan and Richard.

The bride's long dark hair tumbled in waves over her shoulders and on the top of her head she wore a wreath of flowers and herbs. She carried a small posy to match, but the crowning glory was her beautiful wedding gift from Lorenzo: a silver pendant, beautifully embellished with emeralds, hanging from a silver chain with earrings to match. They were stunning and complimented the colours of her dress perfectly.

When they arrived at Holyfield Hall, Lady Eleanor met them at the door and gasped at the sight of the beautiful bride as she carefully stepped down from the coach. Edmund, meanwhile, waited with the groom in the parlour. Lorenzo couldn't keep still; he'd been pacing up and down since his arrival, despite Edmund's best efforts to calm him. This was the same man who had faced overwhelming odds, without any trace of fear, some months earlier when he had taken on several men single-handedly with just his sword for protection. Yet all of that paled into insignificance in comparison to this, his wedding day. He was experiencing nerves he had never felt before and was unsure of how to cope with them.

He had dressed magnificently for the occasion in a red satin doublet jacket with matching knee breeches and highly polished knee length black leather boots. His jacket was decorated with silver thread and the neck and cuffs edged with lace; a double row of silver buttons ran down the front of the doublet. Lorenzo had also neatly trimmed his unruly hair, beard and moustache. He was every bit as handsome as his bride was beautiful.

And beautiful she was. Lorenzo was awestruck when Francesca entered the room. "Oh, Francesca, you are the most beautiful woman in the world," he exclaimed, beaming at her happy face.

As they made their way to the tiny church Richard smiled at Joan, knowing that he was already married to the loveliest woman in the world. Her pregnancy had enhanced her already considerable natural beauty. His smile melted her heart as usual and she responded with a tender smile of her own. As Lorenzo and Francesca took their vows before the minister, Richard and Joan remembered their own hasty and unconventional wedding on board Edmund's ship, The Bonaventure, before she sailed to the New World. Richard wondered if his wife regretted not having a proper wedding with friends, family and feasting while wearing a beautiful dress such as Francesca had, but when he looked into her warm hazel eyes the love he saw reflected there reassured him that she was very happy with the way things were.

Tears were shed when the happy couple were pronounced man and wife. After all the congratulations and well wishes for the future, the group adjourned to the dining room. Eleanor had arranged a feast of a wedding breakfast even though only seven people would partake of the meal. Course after course of delicious food arrived at the table, along with a steady supply of good wine to wash it down. The happy conversation helped the meal along and a joyous time was had by all.

When the minister left after the meal another hour of yet more wine and merry chit-chat was had in the parlour before the newlyweds left in the coach for their new home. Richard's coachman would return to the Hall later to collect his master and mistress to convey them back to their manor, where Richard's young cousin Adam would be waiting for their return.

Adam was a recent addition to their family group and was training as a shipping clerk in Richard's Topsham office. Richard needed the help. Edmund had turned over complete control of the shipping business to him after the successful launch of the first ocean-going vessel. Since then, Richard had acquired another ship, The Eleanor Joan, and a third was due to be built later in the year. Luckily Adam was a bright lad and was learning his new duties from Richard's head clerk Hubert as quickly as Hubert could teach him. This was particularly important because

Richard needed to open an office in London, where his ships docked upon their return from the New World. With Hubert set to take charge of the London office within the next few months, Richard needed Adam to be proficient enough to run the Topsham office while he and Hubert were in London. He was also thinking ahead to the birth of the baby. He hoped to be able to spend time with Joan and their child without having to worry about his business.

Joan was very fond of Adam, but sometimes his enthusiasm overwhelmed her, especially given her condition. Richard sensed when that happened and would take Adam off for an hour of sword practice or even a walk around the garden. As Adam would be spending some of his time on, or about, the dock while working at the shipping office, Richard had begun to teach him how to handle a sword in self-defence. Although it wouldn't be enough to hold off a determined assailant, it would deter any ordinary seaman from causing him trouble.

As for Joan, her pregnancy was proceeding well. Not long after the wedding she felt the baby move for the first time. Soon followed by another craving, this time for quince marmalade. The marmalade could be cut into chunks and eaten as a sweet, but the manor had long since run out of the last batch made at the end of the season. When Richard returned home to the manor after a day of working in his office, he was swiftly sent off to

Holyfield Hall to see if his mother still had any left in her supplies.

As usual Eleanor was pleased to see her son and thrilled to hear his news about baby's movement. Fortunately, she had a small batch of the quince marmalade left but warned Richard that Joan would need to eat it very sparingly as there would be no more until late autumn.

"Mother, I'm worried about Joan," Richard suddenly announced.

"There's no need to worry," Eleanor reassured him. "All mothers-to-be get strange cravings. It's quite normal."

"I'm worried about the birth. I love her so much, but many women don't survive childbirth, do they? What if something should go wrong? It would be all my fault."

"It takes two to make a baby, Richard, and Joan is proud and happy to be carrying yours. If she thinks you are worrying, she'll start to worry too, and that will do her no good at all. She will have the best of midwives and I will be with her too when the time comes." Eleanor gave him a quick hug and a peck on the cheek. "Go home and look forward to the birth of the little one and give Joan all the love and reassurance she needs just now."

Richard arrived back at the manor with the precious batch of quince marmalade but as he watched Joan eat her supper, he knew that if anything happened to her, he wouldn't want to go on living without her.

Still, he tried to put his mother's words into action, and he was elated when he felt the babe move as he rested his hand on his wife's stomach one evening. That made everything real, and he began to look forward to the birth with more confidence, despite the nagging doubt that still lingered in the back of his mind. They would sit in the evenings and imagine how things would be if it was a boy or if it was a girl and talked about their own childhoods. It was agreed that Joan would have much more involvement in the child's upbringing than that of her mother with her and her brother. It was a happy time for them but Richard was dreading the day he would have to leave Joan to go to London. The phrase 'time and tide wait for no man' was particularly pertinent now. Richard's ships would be setting sail for home very soon and with luck the tides would bring them back speedily and safely. Hopefully they would have holds full of profitable cargo. However, before then he needed to open an office close to the wharf where his ships berthed. He would also have to find somewhere suitable for Hubert to live. This would all take time, but barring any unforeseen snags Richard felt certain he would be home in good time for Joan's confinement.

As the time for Richard's departure drew nearer Joan became more pensive. His presence gave her the courage to cope; she hadn't told him just how apprehensive she was about the coming birth as she hadn't wanted to worry him when he had to go away. She understood why he had to go to London, but she so wanted him to stay with her.

"You will be back before the baby comes, won't you?" Joan asked him, trying not to sound desperate.

"Of, course! I'll be back in plenty of time, even allowing for the ships to be a little late," he replied, hoping against hope that nothing unexpected would delay him.

# CHAPTER 2

Richard and Hubert left for London on a warm, sunny morning, after an emotional send-off. While Hubert was touched that his father had come to say goodbye, a tearful Joan had clung on to Richard until Eleanor carefully persuaded her to let him go. Richard shared Joan's anguish but was heartened by the knowledge that his mother would stay with her until he returned.

In stark contrast to some of Richard's past journeys, he and Hubert reached London without any issue. Hubert's first impressions of the great city echoed Richard's: amazement at its size and the never-ending press of people in the main thoroughfare, the incredible destitution he saw everywhere and the stench which almost overpowered him. Like Richard he had witnessed deprivation in Topsham and Exeter, but nothing on this scale.

They secured rooms at Richard's usual inn and after refreshing themselves they decided to waste no time in setting off to find living quarters for Hubert, along with a suitable premise for the new office. The first task proved surprisingly easy. At their inn the landlord had given them the name and address of Mr. Wilmot, a landlord with property for let on the second floor of a three-storey building not far from the river. As Mr. Wilmot showed them the house, they found it to be situated in a reasonably respectable district, with space more than adequate for a single man. Better yet, the furniture was in good repair, and the rooms clean. A price was agreed, and the first month's rent paid.

Richard was relieved to have the housing issue resolved so quickly. Hubert was also feeling very pleased with himself too. He no longer had to rely on his parents for his bed and board, but now had a place of his own. Not only that, but soon he would oversee the running of a shipping office in London. It was beyond his wildest dreams and he was determined to prove himself and make it a success for Sir Richard.

Unfortunately, finding a suitable office proved far more difficult. Richard and Hubert walked mile after mile looking for property to rent near the wharf, or as a last resort, to buy along the river. They even considered places further away than they would have liked, but nothing matched their needs. Richard asked around in the local taverns but none of his enquiries had met with any success, leaving him anxious and frustrated. Time was passing and his ships would be returning soon. He needed an operational base before they berthed with what he hoped would be sizeable cargoes. He was also conscious of the promise he had made to Joan.

While Hubert was off making some purchases for his new home, Richard kept up the search. He was standing on the wharf and staring out over the water when he heard footsteps on the dock behind him. He turned and noticed a man heading purposefully his way. "It is Sir Richard Lovell, isn't it?" the man asked him. "The owner of The Bonaventure?"

"I am. And you are, sir?"

"Mr Samuel Clifford, at your service, sir."

Richard shook Clifford's proffered hand. "Do I know you?"

"No, sir. I was one of the gentlemen who bought the last of your cargo after your ship's previous voyage," Clifford answered. "I believe it was your father I dealt with on that occasion."

"Yes, it was. I was detained on other business in Topsham."

"I see. Well, I made a few inquiries to ascertain your identity, and since you are here in London, I imagine your ship must be due to arrive shortly."

"Yes, she is!" Richard replied. "My two ships in fact: The Bonaventure and The Eleanor Joan. I'd hoped to have an office open here in London before they arrived but I'm afraid the type of premises I'm looking for seems to be very scarce."

Clifford perked up. "Would you consider a warehouse with an office attached?"

"I hadn't contemplated a warehouse as well," Richard said. "It would be worth giving it some thought, however, as it would be handy to have somewhere of my own to store unsold stock until a buyer is found, as well as a place to gather the outgoing cargo."

"I have bought a new storage facility closer to where I do my business and was planning to put my current premises up for sale within days," Clifford said. "If you are interested, perhaps we can come to some sort of a mutual agreement."

"Mutual in what respect?" asked Richard warily.

"The next time you sell your cargo I would like to have first option on buying."

"I'm sorry, but that won't be possible," Richard told him regretfully. "The best I could do for you would be to send word when the ships dock. I could then arrange for you to join my main buyers, and you would be able to bid alongside them on an equal footing."

It had to be this way. Richard certainly did not want to ruffle the feathers of his most influential purchasers by allowing someone else to cream off the best of the cargo.

"That sounds fair enough! I'd happily settle for that!" Clifford assured him. "Would you like to come with me to inspect the property and decide if it would meet your needs? If it is suitable, I could offer it to you considerably cheaper than you would pay on the open market."

Richard confirmed his interest and they set off. They hadn't walked very far when Clifford stopped in front of a sizeable property less than two hundred yards from the wharf. Richard and Hubert had passed by the property previously but the lack of activity hadn't registered. Richard was impressed, and not just by the location: the office was more than spacious enough, and the warehouse would do nicely. By the time the tour was complete Richard had made up his mind to take it. They quickly agreed terms and Clifford arranged to meet Richard at the inn early the following morning to sign the paperwork.

Richard looked forward to telling Hubert that they now had an office and a warehouse when they met for their meal later. Richard held their supper back for as long as he could but Hubert never turned up. Richard was surprised and a little disappointed but assumed that something in the city had caught the lad's attention and caused him to forget his evening appointment. After all, it was the first time Hubert had ever been in London, and there was a lot to be distracted by. He was sure he'd see Hubert bright and early the following morning.

That wasn't to be. Clifford arrived as arranged, but there was still no sign of Hubert. Richard felt the first stirrings of concern for his clerk's welfare. As soon as he concluded his business with Clifford he went to Hubert's rooms but got no response to his knock. He was even more dismayed to hear from the family on the ground floor that they hadn't seen Hubert since the previous afternoon.

Richard was now very worried. He set out to look for a constable or a member of the watch. At the second tavern he called at he came across a watchman who had been on patrol the previous night. The watchman told Richard It had been a relatively quiet night with only one nasty incident to report: a young man found stabbed and bleeding in an alley off the main thoroughfare. He'd been beaten, robbed and left for dead. Although his stab wound wasn't life threatening it was serious enough to require hospital treatment but if one of the patrol hadn't stepped into the alley to relieve himself the boy would have been left undiscovered and bled to death. Since the lad had nothing of value to pay for his care he'd been taken to the hospital of the poor, St. Bartholomew's.

Richard gave the watchman a few coins for his trouble and after getting directions set off for the hospital as fast as he could. He was torn between relief and concern when he discovered that the young stabbing victim had indeed been Hubert. The nurse brought Richard to where Hubert sat on a cot, in an overcrowded room. As Richard walked towards him, he could see that the lad's face was badly bruised, and his arm in a sling. Richard collected a stool and sat down opposite him.

Hubert was overjoyed to see Richard, but weak from loss of blood and still in shock over his ordeal. He told Richard he'd been attacked on his way to meet him for supper. It had still been daylight when two men had leapt out in front of him from a particularly gloomy alley. One of them brandished a knife and demanded money. Without any means to defend himself, Hubert immediately handed over his purse containing what little he had left after his morning expenditure.

The other man then tried to rip his jacket from his back. Hubert had resisted as best he could and had been rewarded with a badly beaten and bruised face before his jacket was wrestled from him. He was still dazed when the knifeman suddenly thrust the blade into his shoulder. As Hubert fell to the ground the men had caught him and dragged him into the dark alley before running off. He was left bleeding profusely beside a pile of rubbish out of sight of all but the most curious. Hubert remembered nothing after that until he woke up in the hospital.

Richard spoke to the staff and they agreed Hubert was well enough to go home, as long as his wound was regularly attended to. Richard arranged transport to Hubert's rooms and left coin to pay for his treatment. When they reached Hubert's accommodation, the wife and daughter from the family downstairs agreed, for a small fee, to see to Hubert's meals, clean his wound and change his dressings regularly. Having done all he could to make Hubert comfortable, Richard left with the promise to visit as often as possible.

As he made his way back to the inn, Richard felt his relief over Hubert give way to anxiety. He would now to have to prepare the new office for business without Hubert's help, and his ships were due to dock soon. With Hubert incapacitated, he would need to deal with all the paperwork and the selling of the cargo himself, instead of teaching Hubert how to manage the job.

The whole thing was turning into a nightmare. He had been so confident he would be home long before the baby was due, but now he wasn't so certain. He feared that he might be letting Joan down in her hour of greatest need, and it angered him because he could do nothing to prevent it. At least she would have his mother with her but he desperately wanted to be there too.

Meanwhile Joan was entering the final stages of her pregnancy and missing Richard dreadfully. She was also feeling a little resentful that her unborn baby had curbed one of her most enjoyable pastimes, morning rides with Barnaby. Of course, Joan still walked over to the stable every morning with a treat for Caesar and stayed long enough to enjoy a conversation with her groom but it frustrated her that she could no longer carry out the smallest task without her bump impeding her or tiring too quickly.

This made her short-tempered. She also found it hard to be still for any length of time. Her back ached, and she could find no comfort in either standing or sitting, yet she refused to take to her bed. "I am not ill, Mother, and I don't need to be put to my bed like an invalid!" Joan said indignantly when Eleanor suggested an afternoon nap.

"It will very soon be time for you to begin your lying-in period." Eleanor gently reminded her.

"I have absolutely no intention of being shut away from everything and everybody while I lie about waiting for this baby to decide it is time to arrive! I am already without Richard, and I certainly do not intend to be deprived of Edmund, Adam, Giles and Barnaby's company as well just because of some ancient ritual. No, Mother. I will take to my bed when the baby lets me know it is time and not before!" she stated adamantly.

Eleanor sighed. She was at the end of her tether with Joan, and she too wished Richard was home—for moral support, if nothing else.

The hope that Richard would soon be home was shattered by a message from London. Richard had scribbled a short letter to Joan, in which he told her of the attack on Hubert and explained that now he would be delayed until his clerk was fit enough to be left in charge of the new office. He'd also added that at the time of writing he still had no firm idea of when to expect his ships. Joan was desolate. Eleanor tried to console her, and Edmund did his best to cheer her, but it was no good. The only person whose presence could lift her melancholy was miles away in London.

Two weeks after Richard had arranged for his new office and warehouse, his ships entered the Thames. During that time Hubert had made remarkable progress; he was able to write again tolerably well and had started working half days in the office. Richard hoped that by the time the ships were dealt with Hubert would have recovered enough for him to finally go home to his beloved Joan.

With an eye toward Hubert's future safety, Richard arranged for his clerk to attend a reputable fencing school where he would learn how to deter any future would-be robbers. He also persuaded a knowledgeable pugilist to teach Hubert how to use his fists to defend himself. Although it was costing Richard a pretty penny, he hoped it would be money well spent. Once home he wanted to stay there for as long as he could.

It took another two days for the ships to reach the wharf and then another one for the excise man to check all the cargo against each ship's manifests, and to calculate the tax owed. The ships' captains and the Harbour Master also had paperwork to complete before the cargoes could be released. Once this was accomplished, the investors' agents and other prominent buyers, including Mr. Clifford, assembled on the dock to peruse the cargo; by the end of the day most had been sold. After a further three days the cargo had been unloaded and was on its way to its new owners.

Hubert had coped well, quickly familiarising himself with the routine and the paperwork that went with it. Richard was delighted, hoping this meant he would be able to return home sooner than he expected. By his calculations Joan would just about be ready to give birth by the time he got back to the manor if he left within the next couple of weeks at the latest.

Happily, his customers were prompt with their payments. Richard gave his clerk authorisation to draw on the account for his wages and any other incidentals that might crop up. Accompanied by two bodyguards, Richard and Hubert then left the Jewish quarter with the crews' wages and a money order to the value of Richard and Edmund's investment returns.

Once paid the crews lost no time taking off on their shore leave—all, that is, except for Richard's captain Tom Ashe, and crewman One-Eyed-Jack.

"What's to do, Tom?" Richard asked, as they stood together on the deck. "You seem troubled."

In a sombre tone, Tom said, "I've told Jack that I can't allow him to sign on again until I've spoken to you, sir."

Concerned, Richard replied, "Has something happened on the voyage concerning him?"

"About a fortnight before we arrived, we were hit by a particularly nasty squall," Tom began. "Throughout the journey Jack had been at odds with the First Mate. Despite his dubious reputation

I've discovered that Jack is a very good sailor with a thorough knowledge of the sea and that he has won the respect of most of the crew with his sound decision making. Unfortunately, I couldn't say the same for the First Mate. He took a dislike to Jack and tried to make his life as miserable as possible. Well, you know Jack, sir. He wasn't about to sit still while being berated at every opportunity. More than once I had to step in to separate them and order them to calm down.

"During the worst of the storm Jack was at the wheel with me when the First Mate was washed overboard," Tom continued. "I'm glad he was with me when the man went over the rail or I think some of the crew might have made two and two come up five, sir, if you know what I mean."

Richard nodded. "Now tell me what you are really trying to say, Tom."

"Other than the frequent altercations between Jack and the First Mate, which were only vindictive on the Mate's side, I couldn't fault Jack's behaviour throughout the voyage. He followed his orders quickly and efficiently, helped any other sailor who needed it and made snap decisions when necessary if the First Mate wasn't present. I would like to offer Jack the post of my First Mate with your permission, Sir Richard."

Tom Ashe was a first-rate captain and a shrewd judge of character. Richard felt privileged to have him as his top man, but he wasn't at all sure about Jack and his black reputation. "Have you thought this through, Tom?" Richard asked him. "You said he'd won the respect of most of the crew but what about the ones who still see him as little more than a pirate?"

"I won't know until after the next voyage," Tom answered honestly. "Jack will have proved himself one way or the other by then. He will either have commanded the respect of the whole crew and proved my judgement of him to be correct or he will have failed. If that is the case, I will be both surprised and disappointed, as I think he has it in him to be a first-rate Mate."

Richard frowned. "I'm still not totally convinced, but you have sailed across an ocean and back with him and know him better than I. If he wishes to accept the offer after I have spoken with him then so be it! Find him and send him to me in your cabin if you would. I'll speak to him there."

Tom took himself off to the crew's quarters and Richard made his way to Tom's cabin. Shortly afterwards Jack announced his arrival with a sharp rap on the cabin door. He came in and acknowledged Richard with a nod of his head. "You wanted to see me, Sir Richard," he said.

"Yes, Jack, I did," Richard replied. "I hear from Captain Ashe that you had some problem with the First Mate which resulted in the two of you almost coming to blows on more than one occasion. I'm not willing to tolerate that kind of behaviour from any member of my crews. Perhaps you would like to explain yourself."

"Aye, sir. It started after I noticed he was questioning every crewman he found alone and out of earshot of anyone else. When I asked some of the lads what was going on they all said the same thing: the First Mate was asking them what their religious allegiances were and what were their loyalties towards their sovereign. Well, sir, I went and sought the man out and told him to stow his questions and that if or how a man worshipped his God was none of his damn business. It was after that confrontation that the trouble between us began. He was on my back at every possible opportunity."

"Why didn't you speak to the captain about it?" asked Richard.

Jack pulled himself up. "I don't expect any man to fight my battles for me, sir."

"Did you see the Mate go overboard?"

"I did but thought it strange that a man who supposedly had plenty of experience of stormy weather at sea hadn't tied himself to a safety line. You'll remember yourself, sir, that when we fought the storm on our way home from France every man secured himself to the ship."

"Yes, I do. As you say it was odd that he hadn't tied himself on to something to keep him on the deck," Richard said thoughtfully. "Well, Jack, Captain Ashe has a proposition to put to you, but I will be honest with you and say that I'm not completely convinced about it. However, the running of my ship is entirely my captain's responsibility, and I will abide by his decision. But be warned: if you accept and then let me down you will never sail on one of my ships again."

When Tom joined them, he offered Jack the position of First Mate. Before Jack could reply, Richard added, "Before you answer, think long and hard about whether you could handle the crew without resorting to bullying or threats! I expect my officers to lead by example not coercion."

"You know the kind of man I am, sir, but no-one in all my life has ever given me an opportunity like this before," Jack answered, obviously shocked. "I promise you both that I will do my level best to live up to the trust you have shown me and try to become the best First Mate that you have ever sailed with, Captain."

"Fair enough! Welcome aboard, First Mate," said Tom.

He and Richard shook Jack's hand.

"Make sure you are back on time and sober," Tom reminded him. "The crew will be looking to you for leadership."

"I'll be here!" Jack said and left the cabin to collect his gear and begin his shore leave.

Richard turned to Tom. "Did you know the First Mate well, Captain?"

"I didn't know him at all, Sir Richard. He was introduced to me by my regular Mate as John White just before we were due to set sail, so late that I was thinking I'd be sailing without a First Mate on board. Apparently, my own man couldn't sail because of a family emergency which had arisen out of the blue, and he'd brought this man along as his replacement for the voyage. It wasn't until we were well under way that I began to have my doubts about his ability to do the job. I was glad that Jack shouldered some of the responsibilities whenever the Mate left the deck."

Richard left the matter at that and returned to the inn to pack, hoping to leave in the morning. However, as he turned things over in his mind, he became more than a little perturbed. Something didn't sit right about the whole episode, but he couldn't work out what it was, and that troubled him. Despite his uneasiness, he knew that Joan's needs must take priority and so he decided not to dwell on the matter for the moment.

His elation at being able to return home at last, weeks later than originally intended, was short-lived.

During his absence someone had left a note for him with the landlord. When Richard opened it, he cursed out loud. It was from Sir Francis Walsingham, demanding that he report to his office before he left for Devon. What the hell did Walsingham want now? Whatever it was, the answer would be no! Joan was near her time and he meant to go home. Nothing—not queen, country nor Walsingham—was going to stop him!

Richard arrived at Walsingham's office early the following morning. He was pleased to see his friend Will busy at his desk, but less so to discover Walsingham absent. Will reassured him that the man was just delivering a message to the Queen and was expected back very soon; the two were chatting when Walsingham returned with Phelipps in tow.

"Ah, Richard, good to see you again," said Sir Francis.

Richard shook his hand, studying the man's face for any clue as to why he had been summoned here again, but he was met with the usual blank expression. Sir Francis sent Will on an errand and motioned Richard to sit again.

"Whatever it is you are going to say, let me tell you that nothing is going to prevent my going home to my wife immediately!" Richard informed him.

"As you should, Richard. If I remember correctly, it must be almost time for the arrival of your child and naturally you want to be with Joan when that time comes," said Walsingham, with that unsettling smile of his.

"So why am I here?" Richard demanded, completely wrong-footed by the man's reply.

"Philip of Spain was infuriated when our sovereign lady refused to marry him after her half-sister Mary died," Walsingham began. "He had hoped that by marrying Elizabeth he would be able to unite England with Spain and return her to the Catholic fold under the Pope. As we both know our Queen would never allow herself to be ruled by any man and now Philip is slowly preparing to take England by force. The Duke of Palma is governor of the Spanish controlled Netherlands and is beginning to bring towns in the south back under Spanish rule again. He is quietly amassing a fair-sized army and there are also signs that Philip is increasing the size of his navy. We do not know when the invasion will come but come it will and we must be prepared."

"I don't see what any of this has to do with me," Richard remarked testily. "I'll remind you again that I am not a soldier. I am not a sailor. I run a merchant fleet not a navy."

"If you would allow me, I will explain what it has to do with you," Walsingham retorted.

Richard scowled and nodded.

"We have been informed by several of our agents on the continent that Philip intends to infiltrate our country with hundreds of subversive operators whose task will be to seek out sympathetic Catholics and anyone else who would be willing to organise uprisings against the crown to coincide with the invasion when it happens,"

"I still don't understand why any of this should concern me," Richard said crossly.

Sir Walsingham, irritable himself now, returned, "For God's sake, Richard, think! We live on an island! These people will be arriving by sea!"

"I don't run a passenger service," Richard snapped. "I'm a merchant, running merchant ships!"

"I see that married life hasn't calmed your temper any," Walsingham dryly observed. "Yes. Ships that need crews. How often do you take on new crew members and how well are they vetted, Richard?"

"God's teeth! They are seamen, not candidates for the Queen's bodyguard!" Richard shot back. "If they can sail competently, do their job properly and are reliable that is all I ask!"

"Do you recruit from the continent?"

"If the need arises, yes."

"Have you recently recruited anyone who has caused any concern?"

Richard suddenly remembered Tom's mysterious First Mate.

Walsingham narrowed his eyes. "I see by the expression on your face that you have. Perhaps you would care to elaborate."

Richard related what had happened between Tom and both First Mates, while Sir Walsingham listened attentively. Upon the conclusion of Richard's tale, Walsingham mused, "That's just the kind of thing we're looking for. I'll be very surprised if your original Mate hasn't been found somewhere with his throat cut!" He leaned forward. "Make sure all your crew members know that they must inform you immediately if they discover someone who isn't all they are supposed to be. We are never going to be able to stop all these agents from entering England, but we must try to discover as many as we can, who they are, where they go and who they meet as soon as possible. You must keep your eyes and ears open on and around the docks and report anything you think is suspicious. My man will be in touch."

"The last time you asked me to do that I almost got killed and Joan was kidnapped!" Richard reminded him. "And as for your agent you can tell him to stop inviting himself into my bedchamber in the middle of the night!"

Walsingham said nothing but gave Richard that infuriating smile of his before he stood up and offered Richard his hand again. "I think our business here is done, Richard. Safe journey home and give my regards to Joan. Oh, and please offer my congratulations to Lorenzo and Francesca. I was delighted to learn that they are now wed."

"My God!" Richard exclaimed. "Is there anything in the world you don't know about?"

Still smiling, Walsingham replied, "Very little, Richard, very little."

Not trusting himself to speak, Richard left without further comment. At the door he ran into Will.

"Going so soon?" Will asked him.

"Not soon enough! I swear that man is in league with the devil! Take care, my friend," Richard answered before hurrying through the maze of corridors to the stables where Diablo patiently waited for him.

Soon he was mounted and at the palace gates, the whole time dreaming of his reunion with

Joan. As he passed through, he noticed a couple of rough-looking characters sitting astride their horses, at the entrance to an alley about a hundred yards in front of him. If he hadn't seen two similar men watching him leave the inn earlier, he probably would have thought nothing of it. He took a good look at them as he rode by and didn't like what he saw. They returned his stare with passive faces, but they were both armed with swords and no doubt had knives hidden about them. The scars on their faces suggested they were no strangers to violence.

They followed him at a distance, almost to the city gate. He was undecided whether to mention their suspicious behaviour to the guard on duty. However, when he turned to look again there was no sign of them in the sea of humanity, so he just went on his way. He was only a few miles out of London when he glanced over his shoulder. Two riders followed about a few hundred yards behind him.

Richard dug his heals into Diablo's flanks and his horse sprang forward, quickly settling into a steady gallop. He looked back and was alarmed to discover that his followers had also quickened their pace to match his. Richard had no wish to play cat and mouse all the way home and slowed to little more than a walk. He prepared himself to confront the men when they caught up with him, but when he turned to face them, they'd disappeared. He chastised himself for having an over-active imagination and pressed on.

After a further half hour of steady riding Richard began to relax. He imagined his reunion with Joan, picturing the joy on her face when he presented her with the beautiful gold clasp to accompany the new fur lined cloak he'd bought for her. The clasp was circular in shape with her initial in the middle and made by one of the best goldsmiths in London. It had cost him a tidy penny, but he had wanted something extra special to give to his lovely wife after being away from home for so much longer than originally planned.

Engrossed in his daydreaming, Richard hadn't noticed the terrain change. By the time he realised that the road was now meandering between two banks of thick forest it was too late. The two men had ridden out of the woods and pulled up directly in front of him swords drawn.

The elder of the two gave him a twisted smile. "Now, my young friend," he said, "we can do this the hard way or the easy way. Dismount and keep your hands where we can see them."

Richard stared at him for a few seconds before he slowly dismounted. The younger man made a grab for Diablo's reins but the horse immediately threw his head up, almost dragging the man out of his saddle.

"Leave him!" the elder man barked. "We'll collect him later."

The two men dismounted, the elder with eyes firmly fixed on Richard. the younger one scowling at Diablo.

"Unfasten your sword belt slowly, and let it fall to the ground," the elder ordered. "Then you can empty all your pockets and put the contents beside your sword. We'll see to your saddlebags when we take your horse."

*Over my dead body you will*, thought Richard.

He unsheathed his sword in a blink of an eye; the leader of the two jumped back, startled by Richard's unexpected movement. The young one rushed towards his victim, brandishing his weapon. Richard knocked it away easily enough and forcefully pushed him backwards. Meanwhile the other would-be robber had produced a knife and was coming at him with a sword in one hand and a dagger in the other. After the first couple of clashes Richard had the man's measure. He brought the flat of his sword down hard on the hand holding the knife, forcing its owner to drop it, and he batted the sword away before it reached his chest.

The young man rushed at Richard in a rage and tried to take his head off with a wild swipe of his sword. Richard unexpectedly side-stepped, caught the man between the ribs with his sword and saw him fall to the ground. In a fury the older man came at him again. They fought each other stroke for stroke until the man's age began to show. Richard could see that he was tiring and forced him back until he dropped his guard long enough for Richard to administer the fatal blow.

Richard was unhurt physically, but mentally he felt a pang; it was never an easy thing to take a man's life, and he'd just taken two. Yes, they would have killed him otherwise, but he wished it hadn't come to this. Now he was unsure what to do. Would anyone believe he'd had no choice? He glanced around and saw that the road was empty of any witnesses in both directions. The way he saw it, he had two choices: either go hell for leather and put as much distance as he could between himself and the dead men before dark or carry on at a normal pace and plead ignorance if any questions were asked later.

He decided on the latter and left the two men where they  had fallen, their horses wandering aimlessly in the road. By late afternoon he arrived at an inn where he booked himself a room for the night. It was a friendly place, with both travellers and locals chatting together well into the evening. Just before Richard thought of retiring for the night the door opened and a man appeared, grinning from ear to ear. The others greeted him cheerily.

"You're looking very pleased with yourself, Alf," the landlord said. "What have you been up to?"

Alf dropped a bag of coins on the bar and ordered drinks for everyone present. He then said, "I still can't believe what happened. I was on my way home and came across two fellows lying dead in the road and their horses still standing beside them. It looked as though they had been fighting and killed each other. It had not long happened, either, as the bodies were still warm."

Richard's heart skipped a beat.

"I couldn't very well leave them there," Alf went on. "After a bit of struggle, I managed to get them over their saddles and took them back to London. Very pleased the constable was to see them, too! They both had a price on their head and the constable took me along to another office where his superior opened his cashbox and gave me this reward. They had been evading capture for months. A nasty pair by all accounts. They were wanted for robbery and murder. God knows what would have happened to me if I'd run into them while they were still alive."

"They would have taken one look at the state of you and given you money," said one of the drinkers, drawing a laugh from the crowd.

While everyone crowded around Alf to hear the gory details, Richard heaved a huge sigh of relief. There was no reason to fear arrest, nor need he regret his actions: the two men were obviously evil. He could only hope the rest of his journey home would be without incident. He was determined to be with Joan when she needed him most.

# CHAPTER 3

Richard arrived home with no more mishaps. He left Diablo in Barnaby's capable hands and ran toward the house where Giles, his steward, waited to greet him at the door. The steward informed him that Lady Joan and Lady Eleanor were both in the parlour. Richard handed his cloak and saddlebags to Giles but held onto the package he was carrying and hurriedly made his way to the parlour.

When Joan saw him, her face lit up. She waddled over to meet him. However, when she reached him, her expression changed and she slapped him hard across his face.

Startled, Richard asked, "What was that for?" In disgust he threw his package onto the nearest chair.

Eyes blazing, Joan spat out, "Because you did not come home when you promised you would! You have been away for weeks and weeks with just one brief note in all that time! I have been half out of my mind with worry about you. How could you, Richard, how could you?"

Richard was nonplussed. When Joan saw the confusion and hurt in his eyes, she threw her arms around his neck and kissed him passionately. "I've missed you so much, my love," she cooed.

Richard looked over toward his mother and raised his eyebrows. Eleanor, just as shocked as he by Joan's reaction, raised her hands and shrugged her shoulders.

Suddenly, Joan broke away from his embrace. "Don't you dare move! I will be back very soon," she told him and waddled out of the room.

Richard sat in one of the chairs near the fire. "Well, I certainly didn't expect that! What has gotten into her, and where has she gone?"

"You must understand that her emotions are heightened at this stage and you must make allowances," Eleanor answered. "The baby is also putting pressure on her bladder, which makes her feel extremely uncomfortable at times."

"The baby certainly has not lessened the force behind her hand! That stung!" he said, rubbing his cheek. "I'm not going to allow my face to be slapped every time I walk into the room, whatever her emotions are! Does she behave like this all the time?"

"Let us just say that she has been a little difficult at times."

"I imagine that means 'all the time' then."

Eleanor smiled at her son but said nothing.

When Joan returned, she sat down on Richard's lap and gave him a quick kiss on his forehead.

"Well, my little hellcat," he said, slipping his arm around her, "have you decided to behave yourself now?"

"You were away so long, my love, and I was starting to fear that you were not going to get home in time for the baby's birth. I get very cross and irritable quite quickly just now," she admitted, and stroked his cheek tenderly. "Does it hurt very much?"

"Yes, it does!" replied Richard, laughing. "If you promise to be good you might find something in my inside pocket."

Like an excited child, Joan reached inside his pocket and withdrew a black velvet bag fastened with a drawstring. "For me?" she asked, her eyes dancing.

Richard nodded.

Joan opened the bag and tipped the clasp into her hand. "Oh, Richard," she gasped, "it's the most beautiful thing I've ever seen!" As she turned the work of art over in her hand it caught the light from the window. "Mother, look!"

Eleanor walked across the room to examine the clasp. "It is truly exquisite!" she said. "The workmanship is remarkable but I am not sure that you deserve such a handsome gift though after the way you greeted your husband."

Joan had the good grace to blush as she looked at Richard ruefully. In return he kissed her tenderly, her aggressive greeting already forgotten.

After Joan once again excused herself and left the room, Eleanor spoke quietly and confidentially to her son. "Joan knows nothing about what I am about to tell you," she said in a low voice. "We thought it best not to worry her unnecessarily so close to the birth."

"We who?" asked Richard, suddenly alarmed.

"I thought it would be helpful if Joan met the midwife before the birth, so we went to Exeter in the coach two days ago. While we were there the midwife examined her. When Joan was redressing herself, the woman relayed her fears to me. You know yourself, son, how slightly built Joan is. The midwife is worried that her pelvis may be too narrow for the baby to pass through during the birthing process. However, even though the babe is regularly active it is not overly large as far as she can tell."

"Just what is it you are trying to tell me, Mother?" Richard demanded. "Is Joan's life in danger?"

"When the time comes, we must pray that all goes as it should."

"Could Joan and the baby die?"

Eleanor took Richard's hand and squeezed it gently. "There is always a risk in childbirth. Joan is a brave and strong young woman, and we must hope that that will be enough to carry her through."

"And if it's not, I could lose the both of them,"

he remarked miserably, just as Joan returned.

Her smile disappeared at the expression on Richard's face. "What has happened?" she demanded, looking from Richard to Eleanor.

"I was just asking mother how much longer I must wait before someone in this house feeds me! I am starving," he announced, recovering himself quickly.

"You are always thinking of your stomach!" laughed Joan. "I will send Agnes along to the kitchen to ask Cook to serve supper as soon as possible. In the meantime, you can pour me and mother a small goblet of wine," she said, a twinkle in her eyes.

"While I do that you can open the rest of your present," Richard said. "It's in the parcel on the chair."

Joan soon had the package open. She flung the magnificent cloak around her shoulders and covered her hair with the hood. Eleanor secured it with the new gold clasp.

"Oh Richard, it's beautiful and so warm," Joan purred, as she admired her reflection in the window. "I feel like a queen!"

This was more like the reception Richard had expected and he began to relax. It was not to last. Joan's waters broke two days later and she took to her bed under Eleanor's strict instructions. The labour pains began twenty-four hours later. Eleanor had already sent for the midwife and Joan had also asked Richard if he would go and fetch

Francesca. Before he hurriedly left for Topsham Richard sent Barnaby to Holyfield to inform Edmund that the birth was in progress.

The midwife arrived from Exeter just a little while before Francesca and Lorenzo appeared with Richard. All the women remained in the bedchamber with Joan while the menfolk adjourned to the parlour to await developments. Within the hour his father also arrived and joined them in their vigil.

It was well into the early hours before they heard Joan's first scream. The sound of his wife's torment tore at Richard's heart, and he was already at the door before his father stopped him.

"There is nothing you can do, son," Edmund said. "This is women's work and Joan will be well looked after by the midwife, your mother and Francesca. You must be patient. Even if you went to the bedchamber the women would not permit you to enter,"

Edmund steered Richard back to the chair. He then poured them each a goblet of wine and they settled down again to wait for news of the babe's birth. Joan's scream had unnerved Lorenzo too and when he lifted his drink his hand shook.

In the bedchamber Eleanor and Francesca sat on either side of Joan, holding her hands and trying to keep her calm. The midwife was checking her preparations for the birth again when Joan suffered another strong contraction and screamed out again. This happened regularly for the next few hours, and although the baby was lying in the correct position it was not making any progress through the birth canal. Eleanor brewed herbal infusions to ease the pain while the midwife massaged the mother-to-be's belly with rose oil. As the midwife and Eleanor exchanged glances each knew what the other was thinking. It was beginning to look as if this pregnancy would not end happily.

By now Richard was distraught from listening to his beloved wife intermittently moaning and screaming for so long. He paced up and down the floor like a tiger in a cage. Nothing his father or Lorenzo suggested would persuade him to sit and rest a while. "My God, Father, how much longer must she suffer?" he asked Edmund, tears in his eyes.

"I do not know, my son," Edmund answered. "We must let nature take its course, which is sometimes nothing like as quick as we would like it to be. Baby will arrive in its own good time."

"I hope it is soon! I can't stand this much longer," Richard groaned. "I don't know how poor Joan has endured it for so long."

Edmund too was becoming concerned, but he didn't dare share his fears with Richard.

Inside the bedchamber Eleanor and the midwife were also worried about the amount of pain Joan was in, coupled with the lack of progress by the baby.

"You must begin to push as hard as you can

when the next contraction comes," the midwife told Joan. "You are going to have to persuade this baby that it is high time it made an appearance."

"I'll try," Joan said, her voice weak, "but I am so tired."

"Once this is over you will be able to sleep for as long as you wish," Eleanor answered as she gently pushed Joan's damp hair away from her pale, drawn face. The girl was bathed in sweat and breathing heavily. When the next contraction came, she pushed as hard as she could throughout the pain and then fell back against her pillows, exhausted.

While Joan was resting the midwife took Eleanor to one side. "I'm beginning to fear that she isn't going to be able to deliver the child," she said in a low voice.

"Isn't there anything you can do?" Eleanor asked her. "Surely there must be something? You are one of the best midwives in Devon!"

The midwife put her hand on Eleanor's arm. "Lady Eleanor, if the baby is too big and is stuck in the birth canal, I'm afraid there's nothing I nor anyone else can do."

"So, both Joan and the baby will die," whispered Eleanor.

The midwife gave her a sorrowful look and nodded.

Another contraction racked Joan's exhausted body with pain, but the determined young woman pushed her hardest, unleashing her most terrible scream yet. When Richard heard her, he put his hands over his ears and began to sob.

Once the sound of Joan's torment had subsided, he looked up at his father. "I'm going to lose her, aren't I, Father?"

Although Edmund was thinking the same thing, he could not let his son lose hope. "Joan is strong and she will fight with every ounce of strength she has," he answered. "You must not lose hope, Richard. You must have faith in your wife and those who are doing everything in their power to help her to deliver your child into this world."

Meanwhile, the midwife gently pressed on Joan's stomach. "I think the baby has moved at last," she said. She continued her examination; when she straightened herself up again, she was beaming. "Clever girl, Joan. Baby is on the way. Just a few more pushes and it will all be over."

Eleanor nearly wept with relief, as Joan replied with a weak smile. After just one more contraction and push, the baby announced its sudden arrival with a loud cry, as if protesting its eviction. Eleanor watched the midwife deal with the newborn, while Francesca flopped down into the nearest chair and let out the breath she had been holding since the final contraction.

Eleanor kissed Joan on the forehead. "My darling girl, you have a strong, healthy son."

"You must tell Richard he is a father," Joan managed, panting after her ordeal. She had never felt so tired in her life. "He will have been so worried about us."

Eleanor made her way to the parlour to give the menfolk the good news. On hearing that he had a son Richard went from being at death's door to the top of the world in less than a heartbeat. He leapt out of his chair, grabbed his mother, and danced her round and round the room, laughing and crying as the tension of the previous hours drained from him. By the time he released her his father had the goblets charged in readiness to toast the babe's safe arrival.

"When can I see them?" Richard asked his mother.

"You must be patient for just a little longer," she replied, smiling at his excitement. "I will come back and tell you when your wife is ready to see you and your son is ready to meet his father."

There was much back slapping and congratulations from Richard's father and Lorenzo. Giles heard the merriment in the parlour and entered, seeking news of his young mistress, Lady Joan. When he was informed that she had safely delivered a son he was delighted, and asked for permission to let the rest of the servants know the happy news. Soon there were celebrations in the kitchen, where all the staff had gathered.

After what seemed a lifetime to Richard his mother returned to say Joan was ready to see him. He bounded up the stairs two at a time and then entered the room quietly, hardly daring to breathe. He stopped to admire the beautiful image of his lovely wife, now with clean bed linen and wearing a fresh nightdress, cradling their son in her arms. With tears in his eyes, he walked forward and kissed her tenderly. As he straightened again the baby suddenly opened his blue eyes wide and stared at his father. Richard stared back at him, open-mouthed.

"I think your son might like a kiss, too," said Joan, and offered the baby to him.

Richard gingerly took his son in his arms, terrified that he might hurt him, and then kissed the child on the top of his head. "He's beautiful," he sighed. He handed the precious bundle back to Joan and sat on the bed, taking her hand. "My darling, you have had a terrible time. Are you feeling better now?"

"I'm quite tender and very tired but I'm sure that once I've slept, I'll feel much better."

Richard saw the spark of resilience reflected in her face and felt reassured. He marvelled that his son, this little scrap of humanity, was the result of the great love he and Joan had for each other.

When Eleanor re-joined them, she announced that the wet-nurse was waiting in the nursery.

Joan kissed her child and let Eleanor take him to be fed. Richard watched his mother and son leave the room before he returned his attention to his wife. "Joan, do you mind if I tell Mother and Father now what we have decided to name our son?"

"Yes, you must," she said, barely able to keep

her eyes open. "We cannot let them keep calling him 'baby' can we?"

"Thank you, my love. Now you must rest. I will come to you again after you have had a good sleep. I love you so very much."

Richard kissed her and left the room. Joan was asleep before he reached the door.

"Well, what do you think of your son and wonderful wife?" Edmund asked his son when Richard entered the parlour.

"My wonderful wife Joan is enjoying a well-earned rest, and my son, Edmund, is enjoying his first feed in the nursery before he too has a rest," Richard proudly announced.

There was a sharp intake of breath from Eleanor who had returned to the parlour. Lorenzo and Francesca smiled approvingly.

Obviously emotional, his father asked, "Richard, are you sure about this? Did Joan agree to your son being named Edmund?"

"Yes, Father, it was very much a joint decision."

"I think there should be another toast," Lorenzo declared. "This one for the two Edmunds!"

He replenished the goblets. When the two Edmunds had been duly toasted the gathered company sat together in the parlour chatting happily, as the tension of the previous day and night slowly dissipated into the evening.

As the weeks progressed, so too did Joan's health. Eleanor made sure she ate regular meals and had adequate rest. When she was fit enough to leave the house, Richard escorted her around the garden and to the stable to see Barnaby and her beloved Caesar. Baby Edmund was also doing well, his voracious appetite ensuring steady weight gain. Richard and Joan were delighted when their son began to recognise them. Eleanor and Edmund doted on the boy and said that it was like seeing Richard as a baby all over again.

Before long Joan was impatient to get back in the saddle. She could not wait to re-establish her early morning rides; she had missed that pleasure more than anything else. When at last the day arrived, Barnaby, her faithful groom, was overjoyed to help her up into her saddle. However, far from being allowed to gallop across the estate as she had hoped, Richard insisted they only walk their horses for a few miles before returning to the stables. Joan knew it would be useless to argue and although she did not want to admit it, even to herself, she realised that she was nowhere near fit enough to gallop at the pace she was used to. Happily, within a week she had worked up to a canter without feeling exhausted and she was thoroughly enjoying riding through the countryside again.

Richard decided that Joan was now well enough for him to return to work. Adam and Edmund had kept him up to date but that was different from being there himself. He was anxious to contact Ralph, the shipwright; it was time to lay the keel for the third ship and although its design was identical to the Bonaventure, Richard still wanted to go over the final details.

As it turned out, however, another kind of business was about to enter their lives first.

Richard and Joan were sleeping when the bedside candle burst into life. Groggily Richard opened his eyes.

"Hello, Richard," a familiar voice said.

Richard sat bolt upright. Walsingham's agent stood beside the bed smiling down on him.

"You!" Richard exclaimed. "What the hell are you doing here again?"

"That's not how you greet an old friend."

"You'll never be a friend of mine!" Richard retorted.

"Very well then, let's get down to business," the man in black said. "Walsingham is getting impatient and has sent me to remind you of your task. You have not attended your office for several weeks. We must apprehend these agents before they have time to establish themselves."

By this time Joan was wide awake and sitting up, the bedcovers pulled up to her chin. "What task, Richard?" she asked. "What agents? What is this all about?"

"Oh dear, Richard," the agent drawled. "You haven't told your lovely wife about this, have you?"

"No!" stormed Richard. "I certainly wasn't going to cause her any worry before the birth, and afterwards she had enough to cope with while she recovered her health."

Uninterested, the agent returned, "You must get yourself back to Topsham as soon as possible. We must all be vigilant if we are to stop these people. It doesn't bear thinking about what would happen if Spain landed her troops here with all the infiltrators and their recruits ready to join them. We would not only be fighting a war against Spain, but a civil war at the same time. Imagine what the soldiers would do to your wife and son. How could you live with yourself knowing you could have helped prevent it?"

Joan shuddered under the covers.

"It would be a terrible waste!" the agent said. "You have such a beautiful wife and a strong, healthy son."

Richard felt the hairs on the back of his neck stand up. "You have been in the nursery haven't you, you bastard! Don't you dare go near my son again! Now get out and you can tell Walsingham he will hear from me if or when I have anything to report! If you have a message for me leave it at The Bush. Stay out of my home in future!"

He'd been wasting his breath. The click of the doorlatch made it clear his uninvited guest was already gone.

The furious expression on Joan's face let Richard know he had much to explain. He hastily related everything that had transpired between him and Walsingham in London, hoping that would suffice, but Joan wasn't placated so easily.

"How could you allow that odious man to manoeuvre you into this position again?" she wailed. "You know how his schemes end, Richard. You've almost lost your life twice doing his bidding! One day your luck will run out. Then what? What about me? What about our son? Do you think we would want to go on living without you? For God's sake! How could you do this to us again?"

Well, Richard thought to himself, if nothing else she's certainly recovered her temper. He drew a breath. "Joan, more than anything I just want us to live safely together as a family. I don't want to become involved in any of this and I know that, despite Walsingham's promise to the contrary, my life will likely end up being in danger again. But you must understand that if these people win, we will lose everything, including our lives. I'm no hero, my love, and I'm frightened about what might happen, but I won't stand by and do nothing."

"Then you must promise to tell me everything. I don't want to be left in the dark if you are in danger."

"Very well, but you must promise me that you won't turn up brandishing your sword like some avenging Amazon warrior. You are a mother now, and our son needs you to be here," Richard answered.

Joan's only reply was to roll her eyes, sigh, and give her husband a disdainful look.

On Richard's first morning back at the Topsham office, Ralph called in with the drawings for the new ship.

"Ah, Ralph, good to see you!" said Richard, offering the man his hand. "You've saved me a trip. I was planning to come and find you this afternoon."

"I just called on the off chance you would be back in your office," Ralph answered. "I believe you are now the father of a fine, healthy son. How are your wife and child?"

The two men shared a few minutes of friendly chat about Joan and little Edmund before they set down to work. They were bending over the plans when the door opened and a man whom Richard did not recognise entered the office. Instead of speaking to him, the stranger walked across the room to where Adam was working at his desk and sat on the stool opposite. Adam seemed pleased to see the man and soon they were deep in conversation.

Before long, however, Richard noticed that the stranger was dividing his attention between his conversation with Adam and what was being said about the ship. Annoyed, Richard said, "Adam, perhaps you would like to continue your conversation outside. My business with Ralph is confidential."

The two men left the office, the stranger staring intently at Richard and Adam throwing a murderous look towards his cousin.

Richard worked with Ralph for another half an hour. After Ralph left, Adam returned to the office alone, a sullen look on his face. Before he had a chance to speak, Richard said to him, "Adam, who was that man and why was he here? You've been working here long enough to know that much of what happens inside this office is both private and confidential. Our clients would not take kindly to having their business bandied about up and down the docks. I do not think that man was a client, so I ask you again, who is he and why was he here?"

"He is a friend of mine, and I don't like the way you treated him," Adam returned. "You all but ordered him out of the office!"

"May I remind you that I own this business and that you are just my clerk," Richard retorted. "I will treat anyone in this office as I see fit without asking your permission first! I'm losing patience, Adam. Who is that man and where does he come from?"

Adam realised that he had badly over-stepped the mark. "I'm sorry, Richard. His name is Nicholas Mortimer, and he comes from Somerset. He hasn't been in Topsham long and is looking for employment here. That's all I know, really, except that he seems a decent, friendly chap who is easy to get along with."

"And how long ago did you meet him?"

"He came into the office looking for work at about the time baby Edmund arrived. He's popped in and out ever since to see if I'd heard of anything that might suit."

"I see," Richard said. "What did you talk about on these occasions?"

"Oh, just general chit-chat about our boats coming and going between here and the continent. Nothing specific."

"What did Uncle Edmund have to say about him wandering in and out of the office?"

"He never came in when your father was here." Adam said innocently.

"Is that so," said Richard thoughtfully. Could Nicholas be one of the infiltrators he was looking for?

After dinner he told Joan about what had happened. Based on what Adam said, they decided Walsingham's agent should know about Nicholas Mortimer.

In the morning Richard left a note at The Bush for the agent. In addition to what Adam had said, Richard relayed that Mortimer was purporting to hail from Somerset but did not have a Somerset accent. In fact, he had no discernible accent at all. Richard also apprised Walsingham's man of his plan to offer Nicholas a job on the docks, not only to gain his trust but also to watch him more closely.

The same night Richard and Joan received another clandestine visit.

"Now, Richard, don't get on your high horse— just listen!" said the man in black, as Richard sat up, rubbing his eyes. "I have sent your message to Walsingham but in the meantime, I suggest that you do offer the man the job you proposed as soon as possible. If he is what we think we don't want to lose track of him. I also think it might be advisable to invite him to the manor and introduce him to your family. Anything to gain his trust and to persuade him that you are his friend. When the time is right you must encourage him to show his hand and then we'll have him! I'll bring you Walsingham's reply as soon as I have it."

Before Richard could react, Walsingham's agent had backed away into the darkness and was gone.

Joan, who was also awake, sat up beside him.

"Oh, Richard, it's happening all over again," she despaired. "But this time it won't only be you who will be in danger—so will I, and our son. How can Walsingham be so callous?"

"Because he is what he is!" answered Richard. "I am afraid that once again we have no choice but to comply. I promise you, Joan, that I will keep you and young Edmund safe."

Richard pulled her into his arms and kissed her. Even as she yielded herself to him, she knew that his was a promise he might not be able to keep, no matter how much he wanted to.

The following morning there was a knock on the office door.

"Come," called Richard, without looking up.

Adam stiffened when he saw Nicholas enter, fearing Richard's reaction. Nicholas merely nodded to Adam and walked directly to Richard's desk. "Sir Richard, I owe you an apology for my behaviour yesterday," he said, without any preamble. "It was wrong of me to presume that I could walk in unannounced when you were obviously engaged in important business which was none of my affair."

Richard looked at Adam's new friend properly for the first time. Nothing about the young man seemed right. His colouring was more akin to the Iberian Peninsula than northern Europe. His attire, although nowhere near the height of fashion, was certainly not that of a worker. He was of similar height and build to Richard but while his face was open and honest, Richard thought he caught a glimpse of something sinister in those dark brown eyes. Or was it his imagination?

After a second or two Richard replied, "Yes, it was most definitely presumptuous of you to march into my office as if you belonged here. However, I will accept your apology this time, as long as you don't let it happen again." In a mellower tone, he added, "Perhaps we should start again."

Nicholas nodded his expression wary.

"You already know who I am," Richard said. "I know nothing about you or why you are here except that you have formed an unlikely friendship with my clerk. Perhaps you would care to enlighten me as to its purpose."

"I had hoped that if I made the acquaintance of young Adam, he might help me to find work here," Nicholas replied.

Still trying to place his accent, Richard asked, "Why here?"

"I've a notion to go to sea and I thought that it would be ideal to start with the likes of the shorter trips that your ships make between here and the continent. That way I would discover if I were suited to a life on the waves."

Richard arched an eyebrow. "Really! How much experience do you have as a sailor?"

"None," Nicholas admitted immediately. "But I'm most willing to learn if you will only give me the chance."

"Adam tells me that you came here from Somerset, but you don't sound like a native of that county."

"No. I'm not long returned to England," Nicholas said. "I was born in London where both my parents were taken by the plague when I was still a baby. Initially I, along with many orphans, were looked after by members of a religious order. A couple who were unable to have children adopted me as their son, as I was the only child there who resembled their own colouring."

When Richard nodded, Nicholas continued, "Soon afterwards they returned to their original home in Saint Paul de Vence in southern France where they introduced me as their natural son. It was only when the man I thought was my father was on his deathbed that I learned the truth. Since the woman I thought of as my mother was already dead, I decided to sell all I owned there and return to London. However, after more than twenty years I could find no record of my past. The religious house was no more, and I didn't know where else to look."

"Quite a story," Richard said slowly. "If you wanted to go to sea, I can't understand why you didn't stay in London. And why were you living in Somerset?"

"I think there's been a slight misunderstanding," Nicholas said. "I wasn't living in Somerset; I was just passing through on my way here."

"But why Topsham? It isn't the busiest of ports."

"I must confess that I came across your office in London and discovered that you also traded between here and the Low Countries and since I wanted to start my sailing career on smaller vessels, I made my way to Topsham."

Richard realised he wasn't getting anywhere with his questioning. The man's answers were all perfectly plausible, suggesting either he told the truth, or he had been well schooled in how to answer under interrogation. At any other time, Richard would have believed Nicholas unreservedly, but not after Walsingham's warning. In a neutral tone, he said, "I have no vacancies on any of my ships just now, but I would be willing to offer you a post assisting with the loading and unloading of my ships on the dock here in Topsham, if you would be interested."

"That would be wonderful!" Nicholas exclaimed. "Thank you. I accept"

"Very well. Report for work first thing in the morning. I'm expecting a ship to arrive soon after dawn and another will be leaving on the afternoon tide," Richard affirmed.

He shook Nicholas's hand. As he watched his newest employee leave the office, he hoped that he hadn't made a fatal mistake. Nicholas on the other hand had learned that Richard was certainly no fool and that to maintain his pretence he would need to tread very carefully indeed.

# CHAPTER 4

To Richard's relief Nicholas proved to be both punctual and hard working. He got on well with his fellow workers and as far as Richard was aware hadn't asked any inappropriate questions. Richard had briefed his captains to keep an eye open for any signs of sedition, but so far they'd seen none. Could he be mistaken about Nicholas?

Soon after Nicholas began his employment it was obvious that Walsingham deemed the man worthy of further investigation. When Richard caught sight of someone concealing themselves behind some discarded old crates on the dockside, he had almost reached the man's hiding place before he was detected. "If you're a spy you're not a very good one," Richard remarked.

"That is because I'm not a spy! I'm an artist!" the man snapped. "I've been employed by Sir Francis Walsingham to sketch the likeness of a man he's interested in, Sir Richard."

"You know who I am?" Richard asked, surprised.

"Of course! I've been sent to sketch your

employee, Nicholas Mortimer, and then take it back with me to London."

Only now did Richard notice the various sketches strewn on the floor around the man's feet. The artist had used black chalk and charcoal on his parchment and the likeness was strikingly accurate. "You are very good!" Richard commented.

"I would hope so! I work at the studio of Marcus Gheerhaerts, portrait painter to Her Majesty." the artist replied indignantly. He gathered his things together and stowed them in his large, leather pouch. "I'm done here now," he said and after nodding farewell he walked away without a backward glance. Richard shook his head slowly; Walsingham would never cease to amaze him.

That was the last Richard heard of Walsingham for some time. Weeks passed without any word from him, nor did Nicholas give Richard any cause to doubt his integrity. The only thing bothering Richard was the man's continued friendship with Adam. Richard knew that Nicholas had used the boy to gain access to the office and then employment, even if his young cousin didn't, but he had assumed that when Nicholas held no further use for Adam the friendship would die. After all, he was still a teenager while Nicholas was in his mid-twenties. Surely Nicholas had little or nothing in common with the lad. Yet instead of diminishing, their friendship continued to flourish.

The reason became somewhat clearer when Adam asked Richard if he would invite Nicholas to supper one evening.

Surprised, Richard answered, "Nicholas is one of my employees and I don't make a habit of inviting employees to supper."

"I didn't mean as your employee, but as my friend," Adam returned. "He is the only friend I have made since leaving Yorkshire, and I would like him to come as my guest. I've already told him all about Joan and baby Edmund and I'm sure he would love to meet them."

"Did he ask you to invite him?" asked Richard, wondering if Nicholas was about to make the move that would prove he was a secret agent sent by Spain.

Adam shrugged. "Not exactly. He just mentioned that it would be nice to meet them in person."

Richard could not help but deliberate for what purpose?

He waited until he and Joan were in bed to tell her about Adam's proposal.

"Are you going to invite him here?" she asked hesitantly. The idea made her nervous. What if her husband was about to introduce a serpent into their nest?

"Yes, I think so. I would like to see how he conducts himself in our home, and also try to ascertain why he has wheedled himself an invitation," Richard answered. "In addition Joan, when Adam is in the room with us I think it would be wise not to disclose anything personal and be extra careful about what we do talk about. He seems to be very free with his mouth as far as Nicholas is concerned,"

"Can't you just tell Adam not to discuss the family when he is with Nicholas?"

"He is young and naïve and I believe Nicholas is using that fact to manipulate him. I am going to turn Adam's belief that the friendship is genuine to our advantage. If Adam doesn't discover what is really going on he'll be quite safe. We will play the innocent too, Joan, and wait for Nicholas to betray himself."

"Very well," Joan said, snuggling into Richard's shoulder. "But please don't let Adam get hurt. He's little more than a child even though he thinks he's an adult."

Richard promised to protect the boy and pulled Joan even closer.

Nicholas arrived promptly on the appointed day. As Adam greeted him, Richard assessed the richness of the man's dress. Nicholas must have felt himself under scrutiny, because he turned towards Richard, "Good evening, Sir Richard! I see you are surprised by the way I am attired. If you remember when we first met, I told you that I had sold everything I owned before coming to London. I am not a poor man, sir. I was very well set up in my village."

He offered his hand to Richard, but his gaze slid to Joan. Desire flickered in his eyes, as he said, "This beautiful lady must be your wife."

Taken aback, Richard introduced Nicholas to his wife none too graciously, but Nicholas didn't seem to notice. "I am most pleased to meet you at last, my lady," Nicholas enthused. He kissed the back of her hand, never taking his eyes from hers, before affording her a bow fit for a queen.

This was no country bumpkin, thought Richard. He was a man of class and refinement, wherever he came from. At dinner he remarked to his guest, "Nicholas, you are obviously a man of means. Why are you employed as a dock worker who is wanting to become a sailor when you could be so much more?"

"I was tired of my life of position and privilege," Nicholas replied glibly. "I wanted to see the world through different eyes."

"And what was that position?" Joan asked.

"The man who had adopted me was a baron. When he died, his title and estate fell to me, but I didn't want to be tied by the responsibility. I wanted to be free. I renounced the title, sold the estate and here I am," Nicholas said, spreading his arms wide in an expansive gesture.

Adam's mouth dropped to the floor. But while Joan smiled, Richard heard alarm bells ringing in his ears. His suspicions increased when Nicholas adeptly turned the conversation away from himself and towards Richard and Joan. They fielded his questions with a polite vagueness designed not to raise any suspicions, but it wasn't easy. If Nicholas was a spy, he was a good one.

Richard went to bed that night unsure of what to think. He wasn't surprised when Walsingham's man paid them a visit in the early hours. Next to him Joan pulled the covers up tight around her neck as usual, while Richard greeted the man in black with a terse, "Well, what is it this time?"

"Did you learn anything at supper that would be of interest to us?"

"You knew that Nicholas was here?" asked Richard, eyebrows raised.

"Of course! Walsingham has had him watched twenty-four hours a day since you made him known to us," the spy answered. "Thanks to your initial vigilance, and the skill of the artist, we now know all about this man. Copies of his likeness were sent to our relevant agents on the Continent, especially those working close to the French/Spanish border. One of our double agents recognised his picture immediately. He had worked with 'Nicholas' when the Spanish were preparing him for his mission here. Our friend Nicholas Mortimer, the latest in a lengthy list of aliases, is a nasty piece of work."

Richard had expected as much. He repeated what Nicholas had divulged about his alleged past when he was with them earlier.

"His father was a baron, but that is the only part of his story that is true. Neither he nor his brother were adopted and far from inheriting from his father he was disowned by him. The baron had his son removed from his stronghold and renounced him because of his violent behaviour, not least towards his younger brother. The younger brother is now the new baron and has inherited everything."

Richard shook his head. Joan frowned, shocked that someone so charming could be so vicious.

"Nicholas drifted for a month or two after being evicted from his ancestral home but quickly made a name for himself as a mercenary and a brutal one too," the agent continued. "He is an extremely accomplished swordsman and a dishonourable one. He has not only killed many men with impunity but women also, and even children."

Joan gasped, thinking of little Edmund asleep in his crib.

"He was soon a much sought-after assassin," the agent said. "He didn't care who the victim of his assignment was as long as he was richly rewarded for the deed. Wealth is his only God and he is completely indifferent as to how he gets it. He has no scruples at all. It was inevitable that he would come to the attention of King Philip's agents, and they quickly recruited him with the promise of many rich rewards for his service. Not only was he a ruthless and efficient killer but he could speak English fluently without a trace of his own natural accent. He was just the kind of man they needed for the operation in England. His loyalty was purchased by a hefty amount of gold coin with the promise of more to come when his task was completed. He was well prepared for his mission and when he was ready, they despatched him to London."

"Good God," Richard whispered to himself.

"Do not underestimate this man, Richard!" the agent told him. "Under that pleasant demeanour lurks a cold-blooded murderer. We do not know yet why he is so keen to ingratiate himself with you and Joan. You must both play along as well as you can and let him believe that you are his friends. Tread most carefully and ensure that you give him no cause to suspect that we are onto him. I can only imagine how he would react if he discovered that he had been betrayed."

Joan trembled under the covers at the very thought, but Richard's body tensed with anger. Damn Walsingham! Because of the man's need for information he had inadvertently invited a seasoned killer into his home! It had put not only him, but also Joan and their baby at risk of being assassinated. Richard was seething. "You can tell Walsingham that this stops here and now!" he barked. "I will not allow my wife and son to be exposed to this man's sword!"

"I'm afraid it's too late for that, Richard. You must see it through to its conclusion."

"Tell Walsingham that if my family is harmed in any way, I promise I will kill him!," Richard bellowed, but, as usual, the man in black was already gone.

"Damn that man and damn Walsingham too!" Richard snarled. "What does he mean, it's too late? Of course it isn't! All I need to do is let Nicholas go and forbid Adam to see him again."

Joan sat up beside her husband. "Do you think that would be wise, Richard? He could disappear and begin again somewhere else completely undetected. Whatever is being planned here involves us in some way and I think we should try to discover the ulterior motive of 'Mr Mortimer's' interest in us."

"Good God, Joan! You heard what the man said! Nicholas is a trained assassin who would have no qualms at all about killing all of us!"

"But we are both pretty handy with a sword too," she said, smiling at him with a twinkle in her eyes.

"Joan, be serious! We now have Edmund to protect too and heaven knows where this will all end."

"I am being serious and it scares me half to death," she admitted. "You said yourself that we have to stand up to these Spanish agents before they subvert too many people and all is lost."

Richard seized her hands, as he said, "That was before I knew just what a formidable adversary he was. I couldn't live with myself if anything happened to you or Edmund because of something I did or was forced to do. I'm frightened for us all,

Joan."

"I know, my love. So am I, but we can face this together. We must put our faith in God and, as much as I hate to say it, in Walsingham and his men too."

He folded her in his arms and whispered, "So be it."

Joan had worked hard to recover her full fitness and had regained her figure again. Baby Edmund was now four months old, and Richard and Joan were delighted that every time he saw them his little face lit up and he gurgled a greeting to them.

One afternoon when Richard arrived home earlier than expected, Barnaby raced to the meet him at the stable door to take charge of Diablo. As Richard handed over the reins he noticed particles of dust falling from between the floorboards of the hayloft. Barnaby, following his master's gaze, held his breath. At just that moment a familiar voice from above remarked loudly, "Heavens, it didn't take me this long to get dressed again the last time!"

Richard threw a questioning look towards Barnaby but the groom was staring at the ground.

"Joan, get down here right now!" Richard called.

"Richard!" she exclaimed cheerfully. "I didn't expect you home yet!"

"Obviously not! Don't make me come up there

to fetch you!"

"Stop getting into such a state. I'm coming!"

Joan climbed down the ladder. When she reached the bottom she made to kiss him but he stepped back, aghast at the state she was in. Her clothes were dishevelled, she was perspiring profusely, and she had bits of straw stuck in her unkempt hair.

His eyes flitting from her to Barnaby and back again, he asked, "What the hell have you been doing?"

"When will you stop jumping to stupid conclusions?" she snapped. "I was trying these on!"

Joan threw her leathers at him. Richard managed to catch all but the mask; as she charged by, she gave him a hefty push into one of the stalls.

Barnaby helped Richard to his feet again allowing him to chase after his wife, now striding towards the house. He had almost caught up with her when she slammed the door in his face and ran up the stairs to the bedchamber.

Richard joined her a moment later, also slamming the door behind him.

Joan stood by the window, arms akimbo, her eyes like daggers. Richard glared back at her. "God's teeth Joan! What was all that about?" he demanded. "I asked you a perfectly natural question and you flew up in the air like a chicken being chased by a fox!! What's the matter with you?"

Joan realised she'd made a terrible mistake. She'd thought Richard was about to make an unfounded accusation, but his manner now made it clear she'd got it wrong. "I'm sorry Richard," she said. "I just assumed…"

"You just assumed what? That I would believe there had been improper behaviour between you and Barnaby?" he asked incredulously. "Barnaby! He's old enough to have sired you! I promised you that I would never jump to conclusions again and I meant it. But you obviously didn't believe me, did you?"

Richard stormed out and retreated to the parlour, where he dropped into a chair. His emotions were in a turmoil. He was angry that Joan had jumped to the wrong conclusion, but also sad that she had doubted him. He'd thought that they had restored the bond of trust between them.

A little while later there was a tap on the door.

"Come," Richard called, expecting Agnes or Giles, but instead it was Joan who stepped into the room. "May I come in?" she asked.

"Yes, of course you can come in. It's your home, Joan. There's no need to ask for permission."

"Richard, I'm so sorry," she said. She sat at his feet and laid her head on his lap. "I have been such a fool. Can you forgive me? In my heart I knew you would keep your word but in the heat of the moment my head jumped to the wrong conclusion."

Richard ran his fingers through her hair. "How

could I not forgive you after you forgave me an even greater sin?"

She raised her tear-stained face to him. "I promise that I will never doubt you again."

They took a turn around the garden via the stables before supper. Joan apologised to Barnaby for losing her temper when she'd had no cause. She was readily forgiven. Barnaby had become well used to her quick temper when she was growing up at Holyfield Hall, but it was usually directed at her brother Geoffrey. He had hoped that when she married, her husband would moderate her fiery temperament but she was such a feisty female it would be a nigh impossible task. He didn't envy Richard.

While they continued their stroll Richard asked. "Joan, why had you been trying on your leathers when I arrived home earlier? I thought that episode had been resigned to the past."

"I think that past must be resurrected, Richard," she said. "I must return to Lorenzo for more lessons. I must be capable of meeting Nicholas's challenge when it arrives."

"I believe it will be up to me to respond to any confrontation," he returned.

"And if you are not here? What then? I must be able to defend myself and Edmund. I also think that you should return to Lorenzo, too. We only just managed to best James between us and Nicholas is even more lethal."

Richard sighed. "You are right, of course. But I

don't want you to be exposed to any more danger."

"Be honest my love. We are both going to be exposed to danger, though in what sense or why I really don't know. Whatever it is, we both need to be ready to meet it head on."

Richard let out a heavy sigh. "Very well. I'll call in and speak to Lorenzo on my way to the office tomorrow."

The following morning Richard sent Adam ahead to the office, on the pretence that he needed to run an errand. When he was sure that Adam could no longer see him, he turned Diablo towards the fencing school.

Lorenzo was preparing for his early morning class when Richard appeared at his office door. "Come in Richard!" Lorenzo greeted him. "I'm afraid I can only give you a few minutes."

"That's all I need," Richard assured him. He quickly related that he and Joan needed urgent secret tutoring, explaining to Lorenzo why and also making him aware of the dangerous situation they may find themselves in this time. Lorenzo was concerned for his friends' safety and it was soon decided when and how the secret lessons would take place. Richard was on his way again before the first students arrived.

At bedtime Joan asked Richard if he'd spoken to Lorenzo; because of Adam's friendship with Nicholas their bedchamber was now the only place that they could speak privately together. Richard told Joan that he couldn't suddenly start leaving his office for an hour every day and then return out of breath and covered in sweat without raising suspicion, so Lorenzo had suggested that he could give them their tuition before the regular lessons began. Adam would go to the office as usual while Richard supposedly went riding with Joan before going on to Topsham. That would account nicely for the state he would be in when he arrived at his office. Joan, meanwhile, would return to the manor with Barnaby, who would once again be privy to the subterfuge.

The new routine began the following day. They all left the manor together, and then Richard, Joan and Barnaby broke away for their 'ride,' leaving Adam to carry on to Topsham alone. The three conspirators took an indirect route which led them into Topsham the opposite way to Adam. They kept to the back streets and made their way to the rear entrance of the fencing school.

Richard and Joan entered by the back door, while Barnaby stayed in the alley to look after the horses. They locked the door behind them and headed for the training hall, Joan carrying the bundle that contained her leathers and sword. This level of deception was new to Richard, who usually entered via the main door, but it was second nature to Joan who had spent months attending the school in secret.

Lorenzo was in the hall waiting to meet them. He began to put Richard through his paces while

Joan went to the office to change. By the time she emerged Richard was struggling to keep his feet and was fighting for his breath.

"Come, Joan," said Lorenzo motioning her forward with his sword. "Let's hope you haven't forgotten as much as your husband!"

Richard scowled at him as Joan saluted the sword master. The scowl faded, however, as he watched Joan spar with Lorenzo; Richard saw not his wife, but the young boy who had saved his life by taking on James and his smugglers single-handed. He marvelled at their speed and the accuracy of their thrusts, but Lorenzo was less than impressed.

"I could have killed you a dozen times over, girl!" Lorenzo shouted. "Your co-ordination is all over the place and your moves entirely predictable! Wake up!"

Joan said nothing, only glowered at Lorenzo.

"Again, Joan, and concentrate! You are much better than that performance! Remember your training! Imagine that you are fighting for the lives of Richard and your baby!"

They took their stance but this time Joan went for him with one of James's dirty tricks. Although he was taken by surprise, Lorenzo managed to parry the thrust away. He smiled broadly at Joan. "That's better! Again Joan, again! More tricks! Quicker, quicker! Again! Watch your balance and your timing!"

He was relentless, shouting at her, goading her

—and all the time jabbing in an out with the point of his sword. Richard wanted to intervene and stop this torture but he knew that if he did Joan would be furious with him.

At last Lorenzo allowed her to relax. She was still bent over with her hands on her knees and breathing heavily when it was Richard's turn again. Lorenzo kept pushing and pushing, the whole time admonishing and shouting at Richard. His student was almost beyond the point of exhaustion by the time the lesson ended, not to mention completely demoralised. Richard couldn't believe he had forgotten so much in such a short time. He only felt a little better when Lorenzo reminded him that it had been sometime since he had used his sword in earnest, whereas as Sword Master Lorenzo used his every day.

"You both have a lot of work to do if you are going to get even close to defeating this Nicholas!" Lorenzo told them. "I'll expect you both at the same time tomorrow".

When Joan returned to the office to change, Richard spoke to Lorenzo, "Did you work her that hard the last time?"

"No, I didn't. I worked her even harder," Lorenzo said. "She had to be the best! Any less and you would have both died."

"Dear God!" Richard exclaimed. "Poor Joan!"

When she reappeared with her bundle, Lorenzo said, "Maybe you should leave that in my office, away from prying eyes."

Joan agreed. They took their leave of him and headed back to Barnaby. Under his breath Richard whispered, "I hope Maisie has still got plenty of her ointment left!"

# CHAPTER 5

On their third day of lessons, when Richard and Joan reached the point where they separated from Adam, Richard noticed someone following them. Once Adam had set off towards Topsham, Richard quietly told Joan and Barnaby not to follow him too closely before he suddenly set off at a gallop. Joan and Barnaby trailed him at a trot, until Richard suddenly turned and cantered back towards them. Just as he thought, they were still being followed.

"Someone is following us, though from a safe distance," Richard told them. He noticed a knowing look pass between Joan and Barnaby. "Am I missing something here?" he asked.

"James had me followed when I was taking my secret lessons with Lorenzo," Joan replied.

Richard raised an eyebrow. "What happened to him?"

"Lorenzo killed him."

Startled by Joan's terse reply, Richard commented. "I think you'll need to elaborate on that later. For the moment, however, I want us all to start laughing before galloping off simultaneously when I shout."

Barnaby and Joan began to laugh along with Richard. He then loudly called out, "This time we'll all start together and may the best rider win!"

All three dug their heels in and set off at the gallop. They led their shadow a merry dance cross-country until they reached the main road into Topsham again. Joan brought Caesar up beside Diablo. Richard leaned forward and gave her a peck on her cheek, whispering that as they hadn't been able to attend their lesson this morning he would explain why to Lorenzo later. He then saluted her with his riding crop and trotted off towards the town.

Richard left Diablo at the stables at The Bush as usual before he went to his office. He threw his cloak onto the stool, loosened his jerkin and undid the ties at the neck of his shirt just as he always did when he returned from his lesson with Lorenzo. While sifting through the paperwork on his desk Richard casually mentioned that he hadn't seen Nicholas on the dock when he'd arrived.

"I haven't seen him today either," said Adam. "He usually puts his head in and says good morning."

Almost as soon as Adam had finished speaking, a flustered Nicholas arrived in the office. "I must apologise, Sir Richard, for being late," he said breathing heavily. "I'm afraid I stayed too late at the tavern last night and drank too much ale. I slept longer than usual and woke far later then my normal rising time."

A very accomplished liar too, thought Richard. If Nicholas had drunk as much ale as he claimed, he would have been in no state to keep up with them as well as he had earlier.

"Very well," Richard said sternly. "This is your one and only chance, Nicholas. Make a habit of it and I'll have to let you go."

Nicholas acknowledged this with a curt nod, but as he turned to leave he smiled at Adam furtively.

Richard left Adam in charge of the office after midday and made his way to the fencing school. He had expected Lorenzo to be teaching and was pleasantly surprised to find the man enjoying some free time in his office between lessons. Lorenzo's concern over the missed lesson increased when Richard explained why they hadn't come. As Lorenzo mulled this news over, Richard said, "Joan tells me that when she was followed previously you despatched the culprit, permanently!"

"It was necessary," was Lorenzo's curt reply. "I will come out in the morning and watch for anyone following you. Don't worry, they won't see me and neither will you."

"You won't kill him, will you?" Richard asked, alarmed.

"Not unless I have to," was Lorenzo's bland response.

In the morning their little party set out as usual. Richard had said nothing about Lorenzo to Joan and Barnaby, for fear of rattling their nerves. Periodically he checked to see if they were being followed but he saw no-one. After they had parted from Adam they set off cross-country for Topsham as usual. When Richard was sure that nobody trailed them, they carried on to the fencing school.

He was surprised to see Lorenzo already waiting for them in the training hall. While Joan changed in the office, Lorenzo reported that neither Nicholas nor anyone else was shadowing them.

"I think the man was just satisfying himself that you were actually doing what he believed you were," Lorenzo said. "He is a dangerous man, Richard, and you must remain vigilant. I have no idea what his interest in you might be but I fear for you and Joan. Be careful, my friend."

Shortly after this incident it was time to celebrate the Yule at Holyfield Hall with Edmund and Eleanor. A time when all thoughts of Nicholas, Spanish agents and Walsingham could be left behind them, at least for a few days.

This year the party from the manor included two additional family members: baby Edmund and Adam, who would be spending his first Yule away from his parents and siblings. He worked alongside the other menfolk charged with collecting the greenery to decorate the main hall, and helped to set out the courtyard in readiness for the villagers' feast the following day. It was a totally new experience for Adam and one which he enjoyed immensely.

Baby Edmund had started teething. Eleanor and Joan made infusions of camomile to rub onto his gums and also used rose hip syrup with a little honey to ease his pain. Whenever Edmund caught hold of Joan's or Richard's finger he soon had it in his mouth to chew on. With his big blue eyes, chubby little cheeks, and curly blond hair, little Edmund looked almost cherubic. Unfortunately, he sounded nothing like an angel when his sore gums made him howl like a banshee.

On New Year's Day, as was the tradition, the family exchanged gifts. Later they joined the servants and helped them to prepare the huge table in the main hall for the delicious festive meal that they would all share together. Adam felt quite the adult when Richard allowed him to drink a little more ale than he was used to at the meal, although the pain in his head the following morning made him wish he had been a bit more frugal.

After their meal the family officiated at the villagers' feast, making sure that everyone had plenty to eat and drink and were enjoying themselves. It was a day that Adam would never forget. He had never been part anything quite so grand.

The holiday ended all too soon and the family

returned to its previous routine. Richard and Joan resumed their secret lessons with Lorenzo; Adam and Richard returned to the shipping office while Joan went back to the task of running the household and tending to Edmund as often as she could, to support his nurse while he was so cranky.

In February Adam asked Richard if Nicholas could come for supper again.

Frowning, Richard asked, "Is there any particular reason why you want to invite him?"

"He's my friend," Adam testily responded. "Does there have to be any other reason?"

"No, but if I remember correctly, the last time Nicholas almost invited himself."

"He just mentioned that he would like to speak to you out of the office environment. It was me who suggested that having supper here would be the ideal opportunity for him to talk to you, not the other way round," Adam insisted.

"Very well, but I don't like my business life overlapping my private life," Richard told him. "My home is my sanctuary and I prefer to keep it that way!"

"You don't like him, do you?" Adam retorted. "Well, he's my friend and I don't care what you think about him!"

Adam was closer to the mark than Richard wanted to acknowledge. He most certainly did not like the man. In what he hoped was a parental tone, he answered, "Calm down and stop acting like a child, Adam. I did not say I didn't like him,

I merely commented that I disapprove of doing business at home."

All eagerness again, Adam pressed, "Does that mean I can invite him then?"

"You had better go and see Joan and arrange an evening that suits her," Richard said resignedly.

Adam arranged a time that was satisfactory for all parties. When Nicholas arrived at the manor, Adam greeted him enthusiastically, while Richard and Joan were more reserved with their welcome; still, the conversation was pleasant enough over supper. At its conclusion Richard addressed Nicholas, "I believe you wished to speak with me privately."

"Yes, that is correct," Nicholas replied, his smile broad. "I would very much appreciate it if you could spare me a minute or two of your time."

"Perhaps we could have our wine in here then while Joan and Adam adjourn to the parlour," Richard suggested. Adam shot Richard a cold stare as Joan ushered him out of the room.

Refilling their goblets, Richard said, "Well Nicholas, what is it that is so important that it has to be spoken of here and not in my office?"

"It's a rather delicate situation, Richard."

Richard considered the use of his name without the title an overfamiliarity but let it pass. He motioned Nicholas to carry on. In a confidential tone, his guest said, "I have several friends still on the continent who would dearly love to come to England to begin new lives here."

"More ex-aristocrats?"

"No, no! Just some ordinary men and a few women."

"Why are you telling me this?" Richard asked. "Surely they can apply through the proper channels to be granted permission to stay in England."

"I'm afraid it's not quite that straightforward. Some of them have rather colourful pasts, if you know what I mean, and one or two have fallen foul of the law in their own countries but only for slight misdemeanours, you understand."

"Really!" Richard exclaimed. "Do these people, your friends, think that England is a safe haven for criminals?"

"Richard please, it's not nearly as bad as it sounds. They just need to be given the chance to start afresh."

"I ask you again, what has this to do with me?" Richard repeated, although he already had an inkling of where this conversation was leading.

"As they can't enter the country using the normal channels they will need to be smuggled in," Nicholas said glibly. "You have ships crossing the Channel regularly to the continent and back. My friends could stow away, one at a time, on those ships."

"You are insane!" Richard barked. "Do you think that my crews wouldn't notice they had a stowaway on board?"

Smiling, Nicholas replied, "I'm sure they could

be persuaded to look the other way with a big enough bribe which I would supply of course!" he added quickly.

"And I'm sure they couldn't! They are all honest men or they wouldn't be working for me! This discussion is at an end, Nicholas, and I don't want the subject raised again or I will be forced to terminate your employment. Do I make myself clear?"

"Yes, of course. I'm sorry, I can see I've spoken out of turn."

"You certainly have. Now I think you should leave, and in future you will address me by my correct title, which is *Sir* Richard."

Malevolence briefly flashed in Nicholas's eyes. Ignoring it, Richard went to the door and shouted for Giles. When he arrived, Richard instructed Giles to show Nicholas out via the servants' door. Without a word Nicholas turned on his heels and followed Giles.

Richard re-joined Joan and Adam in the parlour; Joan looked at him questioningly but said nothing.

"Where's Nicholas?" asked Adam.

His expression impassive, Richard answered, "He's gone."

"You've sent him away, haven't you?" Adam charged.

"Yes, I have, and I don't want to see him in this house again!"

Joan looked her husband in surprise. They'd

agreed to nurture some kind of a friendship with Nicholas to fulfil Walsingham's request.

Furious, Adam challenged, "It must have something to do with what you were talking about! What were you discussing?"

"That, young man, is none of your business, and yes it was the reason I asked him to leave."

"You never even let him say goodbye!" Adam shouted. "Just because you don't like him you've sent him away at the first opportunity! I hate you Richard! I wish I'd never even met you!"

"Go to your room, Adam," Richard snapped, "and stay there until you can act less like a silly schoolboy and more like a responsible adult!"

The lad stormed out of the parlour, slamming the door behind him.

Richard explained to Joan what Nicholas had wanted. Although she understood Richard's response, fear gripped her. From what they knew of Nicholas, he was not a man to take failure lightly. "What do you think he will do now you have refused to co-operate?" she asked Richard.

He shook his head. "I don't know but whatever it is it won't be pleasant. We are going to have to be on our guard all the time from now on!"

The next morning the little group left the manor together as usual, but Adam was still sulking. He hardly spoke to Richard at the office, and Richard made no effort to heal the breach.

A little before midday Richard left a note at The

Bush for Walsingham's man. In it he related how Nicholas had wanted him to smuggle people from the continent to England on his ships. He could only assume that these 'friends' of Nicholas would be Spanish agents.

When he returned to the office Adam was preparing to leave.

"Where are you going?" Richard asked him.

"I'm meeting Nicholas on the dock for something to eat before he has to return to his work."

"Look, Adam," Richard began, but Adam cut him off with, "you said he wasn't to come to the house again. You never said anything about my meeting him here! I'm going, and you can't stop me!"

Richard was about to demand Adam stay in the office, but then thought the better of it. After all, the position the boy found himself in was through no fault of his own. He'd been cleverly used by someone he believed was his friend, and to keep him safe Richard had to let him continue thinking that. If Adam knew the truth his life would be in danger too. Also. if he was honest, wasn't he also using Adam? As long as Nicholas kept up the pretence of his friendship with Adam, Richard at least knew the man was still in Topsham and not spreading his poison elsewhere.

Another month passed and Nicholas made no attempt to speak to Richard again. He didn't even call into the office to talk to Adam, although Richard knew that they met each other occasionally on the dock or in the town.

No one, it seemed, had any suspicions about Nicholas. Richard's captains only had praise for the man: he was a hard worker, punctual, did as he was told and kept himself to himself. Richard wasn't so easily convinced. He wondered what was really going on under that almost perfect façade.

Had Nicholas found another way to get his friends across the Channel? Perhaps he no longer needed Richard for his plans. Nor had Richard heard from Walsingham's man for weeks now. This could mean his part in this conspiracy had ended; Richard certainly hoped so. Yet if that was the case, why was Nicholas still working on the dock? It had to be part of his plan. But what plan?

Richard's thoughts turned towards the return of his ships from America. He expected them to be on their way home by now, and if not, then very close to leaving. His captains wouldn't put to sea in bad weather, but the worst of the winter storms were over. He hoped that Hubert would be able to manage everything himself. Richard had no wish return to London so soon.

As Adam became more competent in the office Richard began to take more time off. He often left early in the afternoon to spend time with Joan and baby Edmund. The doting parents loved being with their son. Sometimes Richard would arrive home to discover that the grandparents where there also. It was idyllic for them all and Richard loved every minute of it.

An urgent message from Hubert brought this happiness to an end. Their export and import licences had been revoked and Hubert was making no headway trying to get in touch with Walsingham's office. He had no idea what to do, and the arrival of the ships was imminent. Hubert begged Richard to come to London and straighten out the problem.

"Damn, damn, damn!" shouted Richard. He thumped his desk with his fist, startling Adam.

"What is it?" Adam asked. "Is something wrong?"

"I need to go to London as soon as possible and I've no idea how long I'll be away for," said Richard.

Adam wasn't entirely surprised. Hubert had warned him that Richard would just up and disappear for days on end, and then re-appear again just as suddenly.

"If anything happens here that you can't cope with, send for your Uncle Edmund," Richard told him. "He will know what to do. Be mindful of Joan and don't cause her any worry."

"I won't let you down Richard, I promise," Adam answered.

Richard shook the lad's hand, wrapped his cloak around his shoulders and left for the manor.

Joan was none too pleased with the news. Like Richard, she was at a loss as to why Walsingham had revoked the licences. They were still following his instructions and had done nothing wrong as far as they could see.

"It shouldn't take long to sort out what's happened once I get there," Richard said confidently. "I'll be home again before you have time to miss me."

Frowning, Joan reminded him, "You said that the last time and look what happened."

"I know, but this is something entirely different. I'll go to Walsingham as soon as I arrive, sort it out, and then be on my way home again."

"I'll believe that when I can hold you in my arms again," Joan said softly. When she held him close, he responded with a passionate kiss.

Richard reached London after a swift, uneventful journey. He secured himself a room at his usual inn and then headed straight to his office.

Hubert was both delighted and relieved to see him. In a rush of words, he explained that he hadn't been able to gain access through the palace gate, let alone Walsingham's office. He'd even been warned that if he didn't stop pestering the guards he'd be arrested. All the notes he sent to Walsingham had been returned unopened.

Richard was utterly baffled. He needed to clear up this mess immediately before it got any worse. He wasted no time before setting out for the palace.

When he arrived at the palace gate he found

the Captain of the Guard talking to the sentry on duty. The officer recognised Richard from his previous visits and waved him through. Once inside Richard dismounted and left Diablo in the capable hands of a groom he trusted to look after his temperamental horse.

Richard made his way to the spymaster's office as quickly as he could and almost collided with Will as he was leaving the room hastily and quickly closing the door behind him. The clerk looked thoroughly shocked to see his old friend. "Richard!" he exclaimed. "I didn't expect to see you here!"

"I need to see Walsingham, urgently."

"I'm afraid you will need to book an appointment," Will told him. "No-one is allowed to see him now without one."

"Since when?" Richard demanded.

"Since two assassination attempts, both of which took place in his office. Now anyone who wishes to see him must have an appointment."

"Well, you had better get me one quick! I need to see Walsingham now!"

"I could get you an appointment, but Sir Francis is away at the moment."

"What! How long for?"

"Two or three weeks," Will answered. "Maybe more."

Richard ran his fingers through his hair, now thoroughly alarmed. ""I can't wait that long! Who else deals with import and export licences?

Phellips?"

Will shook his head. "He just breaks and invents codes."

"Who else then?"

"Cecil occasionally, but he's away on the Queen's business."

"God's teeth, Will!" Richard said, exasperated. "Surely Walsingham doesn't write out all the licences personally."

"They, together with many other things, are prepared in another office and then sent for Walsingham to sign," Will replied.

"Take me to this office, Will. I must get my licences returned and quickly."

"I'm sorry, but nobody gets into that office apart from the scribes who work there, Walsingham and Cecil," Will said. "I'm not allowed anywhere near it."

"That's it? Just hang about until Walsingham decides to come back? I haven't got time for all this nonsense, Will!" Richard snapped.

He stormed away without another word leaving Will staring after him open-mouthed and slightly alarmed.

Richard collected Diablo from the stables and made for the palace gate. When he reached it, the Captain of the Guard remarked, "That was quick!"

"A completely wasted journey!" Richard complained.

Concerned, the Captain asked in a raised voice as Richard passed through, "Is there anything I can do?"

"You could get a message to me when Walsingham finally decides to return," Richard shouted over his shoulder not breaking stride.

"Back from where?" called out the puzzled man, but Richard was already out of earshot.

On his way to the wharf Richard tried to think of a way out of this ridiculous situation. He couldn't hang about Walsingham's office awaiting the spymaster's return, and he couldn't keep the loaded ships in port indefinitely. If the ships were prevented from unloading, his investors would lose a great deal of money, and that included him and his father. Much of the anticipated profit was already earmarked for the new ship build. The situation was turning into a nightmare.

Richard considered asking for an audience with the Queen, given that she was one of the main investors. Yet almost as soon as he had the idea, he dismissed it. Elizabeth wished to remain anonymous and would deny all knowledge of the matter. She would also be furious that he had been so presumptuous as to approach her.

If only Richard could understand why Walsingham had revoked the licences. Unless Walsingham returned quickly Richard would have two ships with full holds unable to discharge their cargos and a warehouse full of goods with nowhere to go.

God, what a bloody mess! And the only person who could make it right was away for who knew how long. Surely Sir Francis wouldn't risk the Queen's anger by impounding his cargos. But what was the man's purpose? Richard had no idea, but he did know that if it wasn't resolved soon he would lose his business and probably his home too.

# CHAPTER 6

Richard entered his warehouse through the back door. Still angry at not seeing Walsingham he headed towards his office. Before he reached it three men stepped out of the shadows—one of whom was the last person Richard would expect to see here in London.

"Nicholas!" he exclaimed. "What the hell are you doing here? You're supposed to be at work in Topsham! Who are these men and what are they doing here in my warehouse?"

"We are all here waiting for you to return from your unfruitful visit to the palace, Richard," Nicholas said with a false smile. "These men are more of my friends."

"The same kind of friends you tried to persuade me to smuggle into England I presume," Richard spit out, wondering how the man knew that he had been to the palace.

"Ah! So astute, and also straight to the point!" Nicholas said, with the same pretence of amiability. "I am here to ask you to reconsider my request. There are now many more people waiting to come across the Channel and I need to find a way to get them all here as quickly as possible. Events are gathering pace!"

"You could have saved yourself a long journey. My answer is still the same. No!"

Smirking, Nicholas said, "Perhaps you would be persuaded to give it a little more thought if I told you that I could get your licences returned to you once you agree to co-operate."

"Just what do you know about that, and how?" Richard demanded taken aback by the man's audacity.

"Enough to know that without them you would soon lose your business," Nicholas replied, obviously enjoying himself. "Surely you won't risk losing everything just because you refused to turn a blind eye to a few stowaways using your ships now and again."

Richard was stunned. How did this man know so much? How could he get the licences returned when Walsingham wasn't even in London? The whole thing was ridiculous and didn't make any sense!

Richard gripped the hilt of his sword. "I don't believe a word you say! I should kill you where you stand."

"So, for the sake of your stupid principles you would not only put your livelihood in danger but also the lives of your wife and son."

"Joan?" gasped Richard.

"Oh, yes," Nicholas snarled. "My agents have

instructions that if I don't return to Topsham within a set time, they are to assume I am dead and assassinate your wife and son. Their fate is in your hands, Richard. Make up your mind. Now."

"My wife is perfectly capable of protecting herself and baby Edmund," Richard retorted.

"Oh, please, don't insult my intelligence!" Nicholas scoffed. "Don't forget, I have met Joan and I doubt if she could even lift a sword, let alone wield one."

"I'll take my chances," said Richard, throwing down his cloak.

"You fool!" Nicholas returned. "You are no match for me and you are clearly outnumbered!"

"Ah, but there are two of us!" answered another voice.

All eyes turned as Hubert stepped out of the gloom wearing his sword.

"Hubert, this is not your fight," Richard told him. "Don't put your life at risk for my sake."

"I beg to differ, Sir Richard. Your business is my livelihood, too, and I also like Lady Joan and would hate to see anything untoward happen to her. You've shown me nothing but kindness, sir, and I now have the opportunity to pay some of it back."

"How very touching!" sneered Nicholas. "Very well!" Turning to his two companions, he said, "You two can play with them for a while, but remember, I will be the one to finish off *Sir* Richard!"

Nicholas stood back while the others drew

their swords and prepared to fight. A fierce battle commenced, each man knowing it would be a fight to the death. After some frantic sparring Nicholas shouted to Richard, "You surprise me, Richard. You are far more proficient than I gave you credit for!"

Richard refused to be distracted and continued to taunt his opponent until the man let his guard slip just for a second; the assassin screamed as the point of Richard's sword penetrated his chest. When Hubert's adversary heard the cry of his compatriot, he momentarily lost concentration. Hubert lowered his sword and produced an extremely well executed uppercut with his left fist. The man dropped like a stone.

Nicholas was in the process of unsheathing his own weapon when he felt the pressure of the knifepoint at his throat.

"Not wise, Nicholas, not wise at all," a man said from behind them.

Richard knew that voice only too well. Walsingham!

A small group of soldiers stood behind the spymaster. Two soldiers disarmed Nicholas and bound his hands behind him.

Walsingham pointed to the two bodies lying on the floor. "See to this mess," he said. Two soldiers hauled the dead man away by his ankles, as another found a bucket of water and threw it over the unconscious man's head. The shock of the cold water had an immediate effect and the man was pulled to his feet and dragged off. Only then did Walsingham say, "Good day, Richard."

"Good day to you, Sir Francis," Richard said, perhaps for the first time in his life relieved to see his antagonist. "I'm pleased to see you have arrived back in London earlier than expected."

At Walsingham's blank stare, Richard continued, his relief giving way to anger again, "I was also surprised to discover when I went to your office that I now have to make an appointment before I would be allowed to even speak to you. An overreaction, don't you think? Surely a guard on the door would deter any more would be assassins. I would also like an explanation as to why you have rescinded my licences for no apparent reason."

"I'm sorry, Richard, but I have no idea what you are talking about," Walsingham returned. "I have not revoked your licences. Why would I? It's very much to my advantage that you keep them! In addition, there have been no attempts on my life recently, either in my office or anywhere else, nor have I been away from London. I would dearly like to know who it was that caused you to think otherwise."

The full implication of Walsingham's statement hit Richard like a brick. The expression on Richard's face also told Walsingham all he needed to know One person had told him all of those lies—the one person he thought was his friend. *Will*. Richard was devastated. Why would Will betray him in such a way?

"Take the prisoner to the Tower," Walsingham

told the soldiers. "I'll deal with him later." As they marched off with Nicholas between them, Walsingham said to Richard, "Perhaps a few minutes in your office?"

He looked pointedly at Hubert, still standing a little behind Richard. Understanding what Walsingham wanted, Hubert asked Richard for permission to go home to clean up. His shirt was smeared with blood, as were his hands and face. Richard immediately granted it, and then led Walsingham to his office.

Once they were alone, Walsingham said, "You up and leaving the manor so suddenly has caused us no end of problems. My man had to break his cover and visit Joan during the day, disguised as a courier carrying an urgent message. Joan recognised him immediately, meaning I'll have to move him elsewhere. This is very annoying as he's the best man I have in Topsham."

"Of course, Joan would recognise him!" Richard shot back. "He's visited us so many times in the middle of the night we both know what he looks like! No-one else in the house has seen him previously, so they would accept him as a messenger. Regardless, I trust all my servants implicitly!"

"Just as we trusted Will." Walsingham drily remarked; "We had to learn from Joan where you'd gone to in such a hurry and why. Nicholas saw you leave the office and spoke to Adam. Shortly afterwards the agent who was charged with watching Nicholas saw him leave soon after you. My agent immediately sent a message to me. Since I knew your destination was London I put two and two together and guessed that you would be heading here. I gathered half a dozen soldiers and arrived just in time, thankfully."

"Oh my God! What about Joan?" Richard asked suddenly, recalling what Nicholas had said would happen to her and the baby if he didn't return.

"Don't worry. Joan is under guard and is quite safe. It won't take us long to 'persuade' our friend Nicholas to get in touch with his people there and call them off," Walsingham said confidently.

Walsingham took his leave after he reassured Richard that new licences would be delivered to his office the following day. After Sir Francis left Richard reflected on what could have happened if Walsingham and his soldiers hadn't arrived in time. He was still imagining what could have befallen Joan and Edmund when Hubert returned. Richard stood and shook the man's hand vigorously.

"Thank you, Hubert! I couldn't have fought them off without your help. Your lessons have been money well spent—you've become quite accomplished in a very short time."

"This was the first time I've been forced to put all that I've learned into action, and it nearly scared me half to death. I must admit that by the time my rival was distracted by his partner's scream I was beginning to struggle. His lapse did present me with the perfect opportunity to try out my uppercut in earnest. I must confess the man had an extremely hard chin!" Hubert said, opening and closing his fist.

Richard laughed. "I think that the next person who tries to part you from your purse will get a nasty shock!"

The following morning a messenger arrived with the licences and a note from Walsingham: The Bonaventure and The Eleanor Joan had entered the Thames and were making their way upstream. As in the past, Walsingham would inform the prominent buyers of their imminent arrival. Richard also sent Hubert off with a message for Mr Clifford, in keeping with their agreement.

While Hubert was away, a courier arrived from Topsham with a letter for Richard. He was surprised to discover it was not from Joan, but Adam, bearing terrible news. Adam had received a message from home that his father had slipped and fell off the roof while repairing the thatch; the fall had left him paralysed from the waist down. His father was now housebound and unable to run his businesses. As such he had divided his enterprise between his two eldest sons, John and George, but still needed Adam to oversee the family farm. Adam would also take responsibility for his mother and young sisters as well as his father's welfare.

Richard's heart sank. Poor Uncle Gilbert, that big, strong, capable man, now condemned to spend the rest of his life as an invalid. He thought of Adam, too, whose life had been suddenly turned upside-down, with all his bright hopes for the future dashed in an instant.

Yet as Richard read further, Adam sounded quite willing to go back to Yorkshire. There would be no sheep involved, and he had no objection to running the farm. Besides, his two brothers would be too busy with their own farms and families to tend to his mother, father and sisters. Adam felt he'd proved he could stand on his own two feet and make his own way in the world; that his father had also recognised this pleased Adam no end. He promised Richard that he would carry on running the office until he returned from London but warned him that he would return to his family soon after.

In conclusion, Adam assured his cousin that he hadn't said anything to Joan and advised Richard that he had used money from the business account to engage the courier but he was sure his cousin would understand. Richard smiled to himself. Adam the boy, trying so hard to be Adam the man. Still, he could do nothing about Adam's situation until he got home, so he folded the letter and put it in his pocket.

The two ships soon arrived fully laden. After their manifestos had been checked against the cargoes and the taxes calculated, the buyers could inspect the array of goods. At the end of the third day almost all was sold. Richard was satisfied that the profits would provide a very handsome return for all the investors.

Once the buyers had gone Richard boarded The Bonaventure in search of Captain Ashe When he found Tom in his cabin having a drink with Captain Finch, another goblet was quickly produced and the three men toasted a successful voyage. Richard was pleased he'd trusted Tom's judgement about Jack; according to Tom, Jack had settled into his role of First Mate as if born to it. He was still rough around the edges but that hadn't affected the way he had carried out his duties.

Richard turned to Captain Finch. "Well, Edward, how did you get on commanding your first ship? She certainly looks well and has brought home an excellent cargo! Congratulations!"

"I have a very good crew, sir; my ship is sound and responds quickly to any course changes," Edward answered. "I'm not the sailor Tom is, but I will watch him closely and learn from him."

"You couldn't have a better teacher!" Richard replied. He promised to return the following morning with all the monies due to his crews before he took his leave.

On his way off the ship, Richard ran into One-Eyed-Jack walking up the gang plank. He reached out and shook the First Mate's hand. "Well done, Jack! You have proved me wrong and I am glad of it!

Keep up your good work!"

A very embarrassed Jack tugged his forelock and mumbled a quick, "Aye, sir. Thank you, sir," before he hurried off.

Richard chuckled to himself.

The following morning Richard visited the palace, wanting very much to speak with Walsingham. The first thing he noticed when he entered the office was Will's empty stool. Sir Francis followed his gaze. "Yes, Richard, as you can see I have removed Will," he said, without any trace of emotion.

"Where is he?" Richard asked, although in his heart he already knew the answer.

"In the Tower, where he belongs!" snapped Walsingham, confirming Richard's fears. "Apparently Nicholas wanted access to my office and your licences revoked enabling him to pressurise you into doing his bidding. His London agents discovered how vulnerable Will was. They threatened to burn down his father's workshop and break the man's fingers so that he would never be able to make a glove again if Will didn't comply."

Anxious for his friend, Richard asked, "What will happen to him?"

"He will be tried, of course, and will no doubt spend the better part of his life in prison," Walsingham said.

Although relieved to hear that Will wouldn't be executed, Richard protested, "For God's sake, Walsingham, he was left with no choice!"

"There is always a choice, and he made the wrong one," Walsingham retorted. "He chose betrayal!"

"Yet he was given the same choice I was—do as I say or I will make sure your father's business fails, you said," Richard angrily reminded him. "Not once, but twice! I went against everything I believed in because you blackmailed me. The only difference here is that someone else was doing the blackmailing. You can't jail a man for that!"

"Just what would the great Sir Richard Lovell suggest I do with him then?" Sir Francis snapped. "I can't let him walk free after what he did!"

"And how many people did he actually betray?"

"He betrayed *my* trust," Walsingham returned. "Other than that, only you as far as I can see."

"And if I refuse to stand against him, what then?" Richard asked.

"He was my employee. As such he must be punished. His career in law is over! I will see to that. No decent person will ever employ him again. He's finished, Richard."

Richard stared at the man in disbelief. How could he be so vindictive? "Would you release him into my care and allow me to take him back to Devon?" he asked, desperately trying to keep a hold on his temper.

"And then what?" Walsingham demanded. "Do you really think anyone would employ him after what he did?"

"I would employ him! He's a good man and a

good friend. I don't believe he would ever betray me again."

"You ask too much, Richard. The law must be upheld. He must be punished accordingly,"

"Which law would that be? Thou shalt not allow thyself to be blackmailed no matter how high the cost?" Richard argued. "But you wouldn't understand that, would you, because you would have to have experienced a real and deep love for someone before you would know just how great that cost would be!"

For the first time in their tumultuous acquaintance Richard saw a trace of emotion on Walsingham's face. Had he at last said something that had moved the man? Did he really have a soul after all?

"Will you at least give the matter some thought?" Richard asked, pressing home his small advantage.

"I promise nothing, but I will sleep on it before I make a final decision. Come back tomorrow," was the terse reply.

When Richard returned to his office his thoughts were still in a whirl. Would Walsingham release Will, or would he carry out his threat to incarcerate him in the Tower for years? He fervently hoped it would be the former. But what kind of reception would he receive if he arrived home with Will in tow? Richard had made the decision alone since there was no way he could consult Joan. Joan! God's teeth! How long had he been away already, and how much longer would it be before he could return? Joan would be furious that he hadn't come back as quickly as he'd promised.

He wanted to go home desperately, to share with her and his family how much profit they'd made from their ships and confirm that his licences had been re-instated. Now he would have to stay here even longer while Walsingham decided Will's fate.

The following morning Richard had planned for him and Hubert to go to the financial sector but before then he needed to discover what the spymaster had decided to do about Will.

Richard presented himself at Walsingham's office bright and early the next morning. After the usual greetings Sir Francis said, "Richard, have you thought this through? Are you sure you want to saddle yourself with this kind of responsibility? What will Joan say when you arrive home with a felon in your wake? What will your father have to say when he learns that you have employed a traitor?"

"The business is solely mine and my father has no say in whom I choose to employ," Richard replied. "And Joan has more compassion in her little finger than you have in your whole body! When she meets Will again, I'm confident that she will see him for the man he is and not the one you portray him to be."

Frowning, Walsingham asked, "Are you absolutely certain?"

"Absolutely!"

Walsingham rose from his stool and walked to the door. He called the guard in from the corridor. "Go and fetch the prisoner," he ordered. He then sat down at his desk and began sifting through a pile of paperwork completely ignoring Richard who leaned against the wall and waited.

Soon Will was marched into the room. He didn't notice his old friend, no doubt because he was terrified of what the consequence of his interview with Walsingham would be.

Eventually Walsingham looked up from his papers. "Well, this might be your lucky day, Will," he said. "Some fool has offered to employ you far away from here and to be responsible for your good behaviour. If you agree to this arrangement, I am prepared to release you into his charge. But take heed, boy—if I hear that you have been in any trouble, no matter how small, I will have you brought back here and you will spend the rest of your days in prison."

Will shuddered. "Who is this person?"

Walking forward, Richard said, "I am the fool!"

Will turned at the sound of his friend's voice. Tears formed in his eyes as he dropped his gaze to Richard's feet. "Richard, I am so sorry for what I did to you," he choked out. "They left me no choice if I wanted to save my father."

Richard was shocked to see what just what

the short time in the Tower had done to Will. He looked thoroughly wretched. "I understand, Will," he answered. "I know exactly how it feels to be blackmailed."

Richard glared at Walsingham. Ignoring this, Walsingham asked, "Are you both in agreement?"

The two men nodded.

"Very well, then," Walsingham said. "I release Will into your custody, Richard. I never want to see or hear of him again."

When Sir Francis picked up his quill and dipped it into his inkpot, Richard and Will knew that they had been dismissed. In the hallway, Will said to Richard, "I'll never be able to thank you enough for what you've done for me."

"There'll be time for that later. Now go and collect your things and meet me at the stables before Walsingham changes his mind." Richard said.

The two men collected their horses and rode directly to Richard's inn, where they secured a room for Will. Richard hoped that now he had his friend in his care he would soon be on his way home to his beloved Joan and baby Edmund.

When he reached his office Richard discovered that Hubert had already visited the financier. All but a few buyers had already settled their debts and lodged the cash in Richard's business account—he could now withdraw what was owed to him and his father, and head home at last. He gave Hubert instructions about how to pay the ships' crews, both because Hubert would need to deal with it himself in future, and to make Richard's stay in London all the shorter. He also ensured Hubert could deal with the new cargo that needed to be stored until it was loaded aboard the two ships, and the resulting paperwork.

Richard and Hubert visited the Jewish sector in the afternoon, accompanied by two sailors from The Bonaventure to act as Hubert's escort on the way back to the ships. Richard drew enough cash for his journey as well as picking up the money order which he would deposit in Exeter. When they left the building and prepared to go their separate ways Richard handed Hubert a bag of coins.

"Thank you, Hubert, for standing by me when Nicholas threatened to kill me, and for all the sterling work you have done here in the office and the warehouse. I'm very grateful." As he shook his clerk's hand, Richard said, "You have certainly earned your bonus!"

Hubert accepted his gift with thanks and promised to make Richard's London business a great success.

That evening Richard and Will dined together at the inn and made their peace over a particularly tasty supper. After an early night the pair were up at sunrise and set out after breakfast. Because Will's horse was no match for Diablo, Richard had to content himself with traveling at the slower horse's pace. The roads were good and the weather was fair, and at any other time Richard would have been happy to proceed at their current rate, but he was so impatient to see Joan that he was finding it difficult not to dig his heels in and gallop home, leaving Will to find his own way.

# CHAPTER 7

Richard's patience was finally rewarded when the manor came within sight. He couldn't wait to hold his beloved Joan, or to cradle baby Edmund in his arms once again. Will was less enthusiastic, concerned about how Joan would react to his presence in her home after Richard had told her about his treachery. He was even less enthused about meeting Richard's father, an old friend of his own father. He felt as if he had betrayed everyone who had trusted him and was feeling very ill at ease. Barnaby came from the stable to collect their horses and Richard hurried towards the house, Will following closely.

Richard strode into the house and threw open the door to the parlour. Joan looked up from her sewing, startled by the noise. "Oh, Richard. at last!" she exclaimed, jumping to her feet—only for her expression to change. "You promised me again that you would only be away for a short time and it's been weeks and weeks since you left!"

Richard took a step back as she came toward him. "Now Joan, as much as I love you, I promise you that if you slap my face again I will slap you back!"

"Why would I slap your face, you silly goose?" Joan asked and wrapped herself in his arms. Not for the first time Richard wondered if he would ever understand how a woman's mind works.

Joan quickly stepped away from him when she caught sight of Will standing in the doorway, shuffling his feet. "Will!" she exclaimed. "What are you doing here?"

The three of them sat down and Richard proceeded to tell Joan what had happened in London. Trying to digest it all, Joan asked Richard anxiously, "When will Adam be leaving?"

"Hopefully not before Will has had time to familiarise himself with how the office is run," Richard answered. "Mother and Father are no longer fit to travel any great distance now and we can't allow Adam to go home alone. I will escort him safely to the farm in Yorkshire and make sure all that can be done is being done for Uncle Gilbert."

"Not without me you won't!" Joan told him. "I'll not be left behind again to worry myself silly. I'm coming with you!"

Startled, Richard protested, "You can't! What about the baby? You can't just go away and leave him!"

"I won't. Edmund will be coming with us. We are a family, Richard, and where we go he goes too!" declared Joan.

"Do you think that would be wise?" Richard worried. "He's not even a year old yet."

"Wise or not he's coming with us, along with his nurse. We'll also have Agnes and Barnaby, as well as Henry driving the coach. Please don't argue, Richard. It's settled."

As Richard opened his mouth to object there was a tap on the door and Mary the nurse entered, carrying Edmund. When the babe saw his papa, his face lit up with a smile that revealed the recent appearance of two little teeth. Richard soon had his son in his arms and was dancing around the room laughing while Edmund hung on tight to his papa's short beard with his little fist, chuckling the whole time. After receiving a kiss on his cheek from his mama and papa Edmund was handed back to his nurse for bedtime.

Adam bounded into the room, having discovered from Barnaby that Richard was home. Introductions between Adam and Will were made and Adam commented on how good it was to have his cousin back again, before embarking on an account of his day in the office in minute detail. Richard was about to curtail the conversation when Agnes arrived to announce supper. Over the meal Richard explained that until Adam went home to his family Will would be sharing his room. Adam was delighted to have the company but Richard wasn't sure how Will would cope with the boy's incessant chatter. Before everyone retired for the night Richard managed a quiet word with

Will and warned him to keep his own counsel as Adam could be indiscreet at times with personal information.

Richard and Joan were in their bedchamber when Joan broached the subject of Will. "I know you have been friends with Will since childhood," she said hesitantly, "but are you sure you can trust him not to betray you again? I don't dislike him—in fact at court I thought him a very good-natured man. Yet do you believe he's completely reliable after what he did?"

Richard held his wife by her shoulders and looked deep into those eyes he so loved. "When I first realised what Will had done Joan, I felt physically sick. If he had been within reach I would have run him through. However, when I heard what had happened to him and took the time to think about it rationally I understood exactly why he had betrayed me. His father's life had been threatened if he had refused to co-operate. What choice did he have? The same choice I had when Walsingham blackmailed me. If the circumstances had been the other way round I would have betrayed him to save my father."

"But can you ever trust him again?" Joan asked him.

"I must, for my sake as well as his. My faith in him has been severely tested and this is the best way I can think of to restore it!"

"Very well, my love, for your sake I will try my best to trust him and will make him welcome here."

"I knew you would understand," he said, and kissed her before laying her on the bed.

The following day Will went to Exeter to see his father. He wasn't looking forward to the meeting at all. He knew that his father would be dreadfully disappointed in him. It wouldn't be a pleasant conversation but he needed to get it over with sooner rather than later before his father heard the story from someone else. With that in mind he had reconciled himself to the undertake the task at the earliest opportunity.

Simultaneously Richard and Joan left for Holyfield Hall, where Richard would have the undesirable task of telling his father about Uncle Gilbert's accident, as well as Will's betrayal and Adam's imminent departure for Yorkshire. When Richard and Joan arrived, Edmund took one look at Richard's face and knew that something terrible had happened. His first thought was the baby but Richard quickly assured him that young Edmund was perfectly well.

Once everyone was seated inside, Richard related what had happened to Gilbert. The blood drained from Edmund's face and the look of shock alarmed Richard to the point where he thought his father was about to have a seizure. Eleanor quickly ordered her son to pour a goblet of wine for his father. When Richard handed the small chalice to Edmund, the man's hand was shaking so badly that Richard had to guide it to his father's lips. Joan was relieved to see that after a few sips the colour slowly began to return to Edmund's face. His voice wary, he said, "I think your demeanour signifies that there is more bad news to come." Before he continued Richard looked towards his mother who nodded her approval.

"I'm afraid so, Father." Richard replied. He told Edmund about Will, and how his behaviour had put the shipping business at grave risk of failing. He also explained that, at his request, Walsingham had released his friend into his care on the understanding that Will stayed out of trouble in the future and that failure to do so would mean him spending the rest of his days in prison. Eleanor was appalled at the young man's treatment both by the blackmailers and Walsingham. However Edmund was more pragmatic. He liked the young lad but like Joan was dubious about his trustworthiness after what he had done. Richard gave his father the same answer he had given to Joan.

"Very well Richard, if that is your decision I must trust your judgement. However, I would caution you to always be on your guard at least until he has proved himself worthy of your trust," warned Edmund. Richard was right in his assessment that his parents would not want to take on the long journey from Devon to Yorkshire and it was agreed that Adam would go home with his cousins as escorts. Eleanor had thrown her hands up in horror when Joan had announced that both she and the baby were also going with Richard. No amount of arguing from Eleanor would cause Joan to change her mind. She dug her heels in and refused to budge on the subject. When his mother looked to him for support Richard just shrugged his shoulders and her husband shook his head slowly in resignation.

Richard and Joan arrived home in the late afternoon to discover that Will had only just arrived himself. Richard found him walking despondently in the garden. He told Richard that his father was furious with him. "He only just stopped short of disowning me even though I explained what I had done was to save him and his business from ruin," Will said. "I fear I have lost his affection forever."

Richard gave his friend's shoulder a comforting squeeze. "Don't take it so much to heart, my friend. He's had a nasty shock, just as I did. Give him time. If I can forgive you, I'm sure he will too."

That evening Richard and Joan discussed whether they should continue their lessons with Lorenzo now that Nicholas was incarcerated in the Tower. They decided to continue with one lesson a week, to keep their skills at a peak—hoping that they wouldn't be called upon to use them.

By the time Edmund was nine months old Will was proficient enough to take over from Adam at the office, allowing Richard to take Adam home. Just in case, Edmund offered to work two days a week at the office and to be on hand if Will came up against something he couldn't handle. With Richard satisfied his business was in safe hands, he made his plans to take Adam home. The almost three-hundred-mile route between Topsham and Uncle Gilbert's farm, situated midway between Bradford and Halifax, had to be carefully organised. Travelling in easy stages would take many days more than if Richard was going alone.

On the day of departure Edmund and Eleanor came to the manor to see them off. After all the final checks had been made and all the goodbyes said it was almost noon by the time the party set out. Richard rode ahead on Diablo, while Henry drove Joan, Agnes, Mary and baby Edmund in the coach. Barnaby brought up the rear, driving the luggage cart with Adam riding alongside him. Caesar was tethered behind.

It was a tedious journey. After three days Joan had grown tired of travelling in the coach and appeared for breakfast on the fourth morning dressed in her riding clothes. Richard was glad of her company as they chatted together while the miles melted away. Thankfully Edmund enjoyed watching the world go by from the coach, while Agnes was regretting not putting more cushions in the coach as every jolt caused her back to complain about its mistreatment.

Halfway through their journey, the road

meandered into a thickly wooded area. Five men suddenly ran out of the trees, blocking their path; two more materialised behind Barnaby and Adam, making it impossible for them to turn around.

"Well, lads, I smell rich pickings here without having to use much energy!" the leader of the group crowed. "A coach, no doubt containing the women, only one man with a sword, two drivers, and a lad and young lass. We will have them stripped of all their riches in no time!"

Richard sized up the men arrayed before him. They seemed little more than vagabonds, but all were well armed and looked desperate. One of the two outlaws at the back went over to the coach and ordered Henry to climb down; for an answer Henry whipped his dagger from his belt and leapt on top of his opponent. Barnaby quickly grabbed his sword, too, and attacked the other outlaw.

Joan and Richard simultaneously drew their swords and vaulted from their mounts before the would-be robbers had time to think. Frightened by the sudden noisy confrontations, the coach horses set off in a panic, dragging the coach behind them. No one was in a position to chase it. Henry was rolling around on the ground trying to get the better of his assailant, while Barnaby was struggling to hold the other man off. Adam stood frozen to the spot, sword in hand.

Luckily Richard and Joan were able to despatch the men in front of them quickly thanks to their superior skill. They both remounted and galloped after the runaway coach which was carrying their son.

The man fighting Barnaby knocked the groom's sword from his hand. He rested the point of his on Barnaby's throat and gestured towards the luggage. "Was this really worth dying for, you fool?" he sneered.

Barnaby never got the chance to answer. Suddenly his combatant's eyes widened in surprise, and blood began to trickle from the corner of his mouth. He fell down, face first. Only then did Barnaby see Adam's sword sticking out of the middle of the robber's back.

Adam stood there aghast for a moment before he flung himself into Barnaby's arms. "What have I done?" he sobbed.

"You've saved my life—that's what you've done, my boy!" Barnaby told him. "That man was about to kill me. If you hadn't intervened, I would be dead!"

Henry joined them, holding his blooded dagger. "Are you both alright?" he gasped.

Adam separated himself from Barnaby and gazed down at his victim's corpse. "Is he dead?" he asked quietly.

Henry pushed at the man with the toe of his boot. "Very dead, I think."

Hustling Adam away from the body, Barnaby took him to the wagon and said, "You travel up here with me, and Henry will ride your horse. We must follow Sir Richard and Lady Joan and hope that they have found the coach intact."

Joan and Richard needed more than hope. Joan's heart almost stopped when she caught sight of the coach careering round a corner on two wheels. She urged Caesar to find yet more speed as she tapped her horse's flanks with her heels. The mare responded and soon they were drawing level with the coach, its horses lathered in sweat and showing no sign of slowing down. Joan caught hold of the lead horse's bridle, while Richard, flying up on Diablo, grabbed the reins hanging from the horse on his side. After much hauling and heaving the carriage was finally brought to a stop.

Joan jumped down and opened the carriage door. Mary had Edmund wrapped in her arms and was wedged in a corner on the floor, with Agnes draped over the two of them, using her body as their protection. When Agnes saw her mistress, she pulled herself back onto the seat but the look of the sheer terror on her face was something that would haunt Joan for a long time to come. Tears ran down Mary's face as she too dragged herself back up onto the seat and sat the baby on her lap. Little Edmund, completely unharmed by the near disaster, recognised his mama immediately and gave her the same big smile he always did when she entered the nursery, none the worse for his big adventure thanks to Mary and Agnes.

Weeping, Joan took the child from his nurse and held him close to her breast. Richard appeared just long enough to make sure that everyone was safe before he went to unshackle the two terrified horses and tether them under the trees.

When he returned to Joan, she was sitting on a patch of grass, cradling Edmund. Agnes and Mary sat beside her, still in a state of shock. Richard was about to go look for the others when he heard the wagon further down the road; he was relieved to see the other members of his party, safe and in control. When Barnaby explained what had happened, Richard let Adam know how proud he was of his courage. Without the lad's intervention Barnaby would have lost his life otherwise. Although Adam still felt terribly upset at taking a man's life, he accepted Richard's assurances.

It was the nurse who noticed that both Henry and Barnaby were bleeding. On investigation Mary discovered that they had incurred some nasty cuts on their arms but nothing too serious; their wounds were soon cleaned and bandaged. Richard announced that they would rest for a while before continuing on their journey to the next town. Barnaby and Henry left the others and attended to the horses; the two men spoke to them gently as they rubbed them down and found them some water. Before it was time to move on again Joan spoke quietly to Richard. "How many more people are we going to be forced to kill? Those men probably had no choice but to take to highway robbery just to stay alive being guilty of nothing more than having no home or employment."

"I know, my love, but those men were intent on

killing us and we had no time to reason with them. Our son's life was in grave danger."

"I understand that but why do I not feel more remorse for what I did?

"You are still in shock my love. The grief will come later." Richard replied squeezing her hand. Joan opted to ride in the coach with the other women and her son; Mary and Agnes were both still nervous after their terrifying ordeal.

The next town was Derby. When they arrived Richard explained to the officials what had happened on the road. Soldiers were despatched to collect the bodies, while the family was directed to one of the better hostelries. They were all looking forward to a tasty meal followed by a good night's sleep.

In the morning Richard received a visit from the Captain of the Guard. He revealed that the gang of outlaws that had attacked them had been terrorising the area for months and had managed to evade all the military patrols. No further action would be taken against Richard's family. Instead, the Captain passed on the grateful community's thanks for ridding them of the plague of outlaws.

Thankfully the remainder of their journey was uneventful and they reached their destination five days later. They received a warm welcome. Sarah and the girls were in raptures over the baby, and while the women fussed over him, Adam and Richard sat with Gilbert, who was grateful to have his son home again. It astonished him, just how much the boy had grown not just in stature but in confidence too.

Unfortunately Uncle Gilbert had received no professional medical help as he couldn't get to town, and no physician would travel so far out into the country to see him. The crippled man was relieved to learn that Richard would be visiting a physician in York who specialised in back injuries, and paralysis in particular. The man in question was known to his brother Edmund, and he'd given Richard a letter of introduction. It was hoped that the physician would take up Gilbert's case.

The following day Richard left for York. He expected the trip to take no more than four days in total. While Richard was away, word would be sent to the rest of Gilbert and Sarah's family inviting them to a celebration meal, where the two branches of the family could meet each other for the first time.

Sarah had gone to great lengths to house her guests comfortably, but she only had Annabel and Hannah for helpers. Preparing and cooking the meals for the enlarged household took up most of the day. Although Joan had delegated Agnes to help in the kitchen, she wanted to contribute something herself.

"When you first met me," Joan said to Sarah, "you commented that I was the daughter of a lord, and you were right. As such I had servants to wait on me from the moment I was born and was allowed nothing at all to do with anything domestic. I would dearly love to learn how to cook. Will you teach me, Sarah?"

"I would be honoured," Sarah replied with a smile. "However, I think your beautiful gown would get in the way and soon be ruined."

"Oh," said Joan despondently. "I don't have any other kind of dress."

"I could let you borrow one of mine, but it would be a little big on you," Sarah warned her.

Joan nevertheless agreed and began her cooking lessons.

Richard returned four days later as promised. When he didn't find anyone in the main room of the farmhouse, he followed the lovely aroma coming from the kitchen. There he found three women busily preparing meat and vegetables. He immediately recognised Sarah and Agnes, but not the other woman, whose back was to him. When he asked Agnes where he could find her mistress, he heard a little chuckle as the third woman turned to face him. She was wearing a peasant's dress hitched up with twine, the front of it covered with a long apron and a cap pulled down firmly on her head.

Richard stared at her for a few seconds but when she smiled and he saw that wicked twinkle in her eyes he knew he had found his Joan.

"What are you up to now, my little minx?" he asked her. "I suppose I should be grateful that you are not digging the garden!"

They both laughed as Richard gathered Joan into his arms. When they had calmed down Joan explained that Sarah was teaching her how to cook.

Richard chuckled again.

"What's so funny about that?" Joan demanded.

"I was just imagining Queen Elizabeth's reaction if she saw you like this," Richard replied. "After all, you did used to be her lady-in-waiting."

"I think she would be a little bit jealous that I was able to do something so very ordinary. Sometimes Her Majesty felt very restricted by her many duties and longed to live as one of her people, even if just for a little while," Joan answered a little sadly, remembering her time at court with her beloved sovereign.

"Where's Uncle Gilbert?" Richard asked. "I didn't see him when I came in."

"Adam enlisted Henry and Barnaby to help him lift his father, complete with chair, and carry him over to the stable to enjoy some male company. Oh, and then Adam and Barnaby came back to collect a small keg of beer and some tankards," Joan added.

"In that case I think I'll go and join them and leave you ladies to carry on with what you are doing," Richard said.

He gave Joan a brief kiss and left the kitchen, picking up a tankard on his way out. He found the jolly group sitting on benches around an upturned barrel. Each held a tankard of ale and were chatting and laughing like old friends. Richard found himself a stool, poured some ale from the keg and joined in with the conversation. Gilbert was relieved when Richard informed him that the physician would visit before the end of the week.

In the meantime, everyone had the family meal to look forward to. On the appointed day Adam's brothers John and George brought their young families and the house was soon overflowing. The menfolk set up trestles and benches in the yard, while the women busied themselves in the kitchen. Once the meal was served it didn't take long before everyone was talking together as if they had known each other for years, instead of meeting for the first time. Joan couldn't believe how comfortable she felt around these people and reflected on all the warmth and honest friendship she had missed in her life.

All too soon John and George needed to return to their own farms and flocks. The lambing season had been a particularly successful one and the brothers were both busy sorting out what stock they wanted to keep and what to sell. As the two families left for home there were tearful farewells and promises that they would all see each other again.

Three days after the family meal the physician visited, accompanied by his two bodyguards. He introduced himself as Hamid and, after some refreshment, proceeded directly to the examination. Gilbert laid on his bed face down as Hakim gently prodded around the base of his spine. Richard then helped Gilbert up into a sitting position, his legs hanging over the edge of the bed, so that Hakim could manoeuvre his patient's legs backwards and forwards, as well as from side to side.

All through the examination Hakim was talking to himself in Arabic or asking intermittent questions in English. His evaluation was very thorough and when he had finished, he sat in a chair and tapped his fingers on the table for a few seconds. Finally, he said, "I have examined the patient carefully but intensely and I am hopeful that the spinal cord hasn't been completely severed. However, there is no way I can be absolutely certain. Do any of you know how to read?"

"I do," Adam said immediately.

"Did you see how I manipulated your father's legs?" Hakim asked him. When Adam replied he had, the physician continued "Good, good!" and took a sheaf of papers out of his bag. "These are the instructions for all the exercises and the relevant diagrams. They must all be done twice a day, every day without fail," he stressed. "Once you both become familiar with them, they will become easier. I cannot promise miracles—you must be aware that they might not make any difference at all. But I am hopeful that there will be some improvement to the mobility. This will not happen overnight so you must be patient and keep doing the exercises."

Even if Hakim could not promise miracles, he had given them hope. Adam and Gilbert shook the man's hand and Sarah thanked him with tears in her eyes.

In the yard Richard asked Hakim why his father's letter had compelled him to come and see Gilbert.

"Despite my healing skills there are still people who don't like having foreigners in their midst," Hakim answered. "Unfortunately, one night while returning home after visiting a patient I found my life threatened by two nasty characters who not only objected to my race but also to my religion. I was lucky that your father came upon us and persuaded the two men to leave with the point of his sword. I owe your father my life, Richard."

As Richard watched Hakim and his bodyguards disappear down the road, he realised that there was probably a lot more he did not know about his father.

But now that Adam was safely back and the examination over, it was time for Richard and Joan to return home. Their departure proved a sad affair for everyone. Joan had grown extraordinarily fond of Aunt Sarah; Abigail and Hannah could hardly bear to part with baby Edmund; and Richard had spent many happy hours talking with Uncle Gilbert. Gilbert's tales of his childhood with Edmund had captivated Richard; he'd enjoyed hearing about the many scrapes they had got into as boys. He also felt an immense amount of respect for how Gilbert had gone out into the world with next to nothing and yet made such a success of his life.

Yet leave they must, so Joan and Richard sent word ahead to let Edmund and Eleanor know that they were on their way home. The weather was fine and the roads good; the only discord was Agnes and her incessant complaints about how travelling in the coach made her back ache. Eventually Joan's patience came to an end and she threatened to make her maid walk all the way to Topsham, which did the trick—Agnes hated walking anywhere. That was the last anyone heard about her back.

When they approached the site of the thieves' ambush, everyone became tense and wary. There was no sign that anything untoward had happened previously; the soldiers had done their job well. When the road finally emerged from the trees Richard noticed that Joan seemed lost in thought.

"Is something wrong?" Richard asked.

"I'm not sure I like the kind of woman I have become," Joan confessed to him. "Before confronting James and his gang of smugglers I had never wielded a weapon in earnest or even owned one. It was the same with the outlaws who were trying to rob us. I drew my sword and was prepared to use it without a second thought. You were right. I did feel grief and regret later but I expected it to be more. I don't even know how many men I have killed. What has happened to me, Richard? I'm terrified that I might be turning into a James Cavendish."

A few teardrops ran down her face.

"Oh, my love," Richard said, taking her hand, "since the day we met we have been thrown into circumstances which were none of our making. If we hadn't have protected ourselves, we would both be dead. We only killed in self-defence; we were never the aggressors. We fought to preserve our lives and those of others against evil men." He paused before he went on, "I had also never killed anyone before and it frightens me, too. It has changed both of us, but we are not bad people, my darling. We did what we had to do to stay alive."

"I know, Richard, I know," she wept. "But when will it all end? Will it ever stop? If only Walsingham would leave us alone."

"It can't go on forever, Joan. It must not," he said—and to himself he added, "I'll make damn sure it doesn't."

They arrived at the manor in late afternoon. Maisie, Ellen, Tom, and Giles were waiting for them; they couldn't believe how Edmund had grown. The babe relished all the extra attention, until the nurse Mary whisked him off to the nursery under protest.

Joan and Richard were relaxing in the parlour when Will arrived home from the office, closely followed by Edmund. Edmund pulled up a chair beside his son and demanded to be brought up to date with all their news. Will didn't want to intrude on the family reunion and quietly left for his room. Edmund was pleased to hear that there was at least some hope his brother might regain the partial use of his legs. He asked after Hakim, but when Richard asked Edmund about how he had rescued the doctor, Edmund declined to elaborate.

Before Richard could press him, the nurse arrived carrying the baby. Little Edmund was in his grandfather's arms before the nurse knew what was happening; the elder Edmund had the baby on his knee where he bounced the giggling young Edmund up and down, while Mary prayed that the boy's supper would remain in his stomach.

Eventually the babe was relinquished to his nurse, and Edmund prepared to leave for Holyfield. "Oh, I almost forgot!" he said, and produced a letter, which he handed to Richard. "This was delivered to your office by a young lad earlier today. He said it was to be given to you immediately upon your return. I was intending to leave it here for you."

Richard opened the letter. As he read, his expression moved from utter disbelief to downright anger. "I knew that damn man Walsingham was crazy, and this proves it!" he snarled.

"What proves it? What does it say, Richard?" Edmund asked.

"That idiot! That bloody fool of a man has taken that murdering bastard Nicholas into his spy network!" Richard exclaimed. "He will be taking up his job on the dock again and I am to allow my ships to ferry his people across the Channel! Like hell I will! I'm not one of his lackeys or one of his spies. I will not be told what to do with my own ships by that madman, nor will I have that snake back anywhere near me or my ships!"

Joan shuddered visibly as she remembered the threat Nicholas had posed to their lives. "Richard, I swear that if that man sets foot in our home again I will run him through myself!" she told him.

"Don't worry, my love," Richard replied. "There's no way he will ever inveigle his way to an invitation again. If he tries he will soon discover that Will is not the naïve adolescent that Adam was, and he certainly won't be made welcome by me!"

"Does the letter say anything else?" asked his father.

"Just that his man will be in touch to go over the finer details," Richard said. "Well, he need not bother! It's not going to happen and that's final!"

Richard tried to sound positive, for Joan's sake. But they both knew from past experience that Walsingham inevitably got his way.

# CHAPTER 8

Over breakfast Richard explained the contents of Walsingham's letter to Will. Poor Will nearly choked when he realised what Sir Francis was demanding. "Surely you don't intend to let that man work for you again, do you?" Will asked Richard anxiously.

"I'd rather not, but knowing Walsingham, when he sets his mind to something I'm not sure I'll be given the choice. But I'm not happy about it, Will, not happy at all!" Richard admitted. "If Nicholas approaches you for any reason whatsoever, I want to know immediately."

"When you gave me a second chance, I promised you that I would never betray you again, and that is a pledge I intend to keep," Will replied. "I am now your man and always will be."

"I know, my friend, but while that man is in my employ I want to know every move he makes. I don't trust him one inch and I won't be caught napping again! Do you know how to use a sword?" Joan raised her eyebrows and threw Richard a questioning glance.

"No," Will replied. "I've never had any need. Why do you ask?"

"I think that taking into consideration the kind of people we might find ourselves up against it would be advisable for you to begin a course of lessons," Richard answered. "I'll talk to Lorenzo about getting you enrolled in a beginner's class as soon as possible."

As soon as Will had gone to his room, Joan spoke to Richard urgently, "Are you sure that is wise? Could that not make Will yet another threat to our lives? After all, it was because of Nicholas he betrayed you before and now he could be exposed to his influence again!"

"When Will betrayed me I believe that it was not only the first time but also the last , my love. I really wish you could believe it, too. I have no fear of any harm from him, but nor do I want any harm to come to him which, is why I want him to be able to protect himself."

"I will try, Richard, I really will," Joan said even though she was still finding it hard to forgive Will for what he'd done and even more difficult to trust him again.

They all left the manor together, splitting up when Joan and Barnaby left for their morning ride. Richard and Will carried on towards Topsham and called in at the fencing school. When Lorenzo confirmed a place for Will in one of his classes Richard and his clerk headed into their office. Richard saw no sign of Nicholas. He knew he would have to face the man again sooner or later, but for now he was happy to delay the inevitable.

Late that night Richard and Joan received another clandestine visit from Walsingham's man. "You again!" snapped Richard, causing Joan to wake with a start.

"I'm sorry if I startled you both, but this is urgent," the man in black informed them. "I believe that you have already heard from Walsingham?"

"Yes, I have! What is that fool of a man thinking by asking me to carry on as if nothing had happened?" Richard demanded. "To take that snake back and put my ships at his disposal to smuggle traitors into the country. He's out of mind! I won't do it!"

"No, Richard, he's perfectly sane and extremely shrewd. He has turned Nicholas with the help of a huge bribe and now the traitor is working for us as a double agent."

"And what makes Sir Francis think that he can trust that double-crossing murderous cut-throat?"

"He doesn't trust him, and neither must you. Not even for a moment," the man warned Richard.

"Then what the hell is the purpose of this ridiculous nonsense?"

"We know that eventually Nicholas will put his head in a noose. But in the meantime, we will be able to keep track of the people who come in on your ships and also on the sympathisers they recruit. When the time is right, we will arrest them all before they can incite any seditious uprising."

"Oh I see, and while all this is happening I'm expected to turn a blind eye to my ships being used to ferry traitors into England," Richard said sarcastically.

Backing away into the shadows, the agent said, "Yes, Richard, that's correct."

"It's SIR Richard!" he shouted after the man, but he was just shouting at an empty space.

A few days after the visit by Walsingham's man Richard went down to the docks and came face-to-face with Nicholas.

"Well met, Richard!" his arch enemy hailed with a mocking salute. "I believe you have already received your orders from Walsingham to offer me every assistance to get my people over the channel."

"Yes, Walsingham has asked me to aid you in the smuggling of traitors into the country. But may I remind you that I am the owner of the very ships you require to complete your task, and could easily refuse to co-operate," Richard returned.

Nicholas laughed. "Not while Walsingham is pulling your strings, you won't. You wouldn't dare disobey him and you know it."

"I wouldn't need to if you were dead," said Richard.

His hand slid to the hilt of his sword.

"Don't be such a fool," Nicholas snorted. "You're no match for me. Besides, I'm sure Sir

Francis would be more forgiving of me killing you than you putting an end to me! I am far more important to his plans." With that infuriating smile of his, Nicholas added, "I would say, however, that if you were unfortunately killed in this venture I would certainly not be averse to keeping Joan's bed warm. She's a very beautiful woman. Who knows, she might prefer to have a real man lying beside her!"

As Richard made a grab for him Nicholas ducked away and ran down the dock, laughing.

By the time Richard reached his office he was like an angry bear with the toothache. He slammed the door so hard the whole room vibrated, but luckily no one was there to witness this act of rage; Will was off having his first lesson at the fencing school. By the time he staggered in, dripping with sweat, Richard had himself under control again. He spent the afternoon tracking down his captains, informing them that if they were approached on the continent by anyone who said they'd been sent by Willum, that man should be allowed to work his passage to Topsham. This was highly irregular, but Richard's captains didn't question his orders—they'd worked for him for years and had complete faith in him.

In the days that followed Nicholas stayed away from Richard, perhaps aware that he'd pushed Richard to his limit. Nicholas also made no attempt to contact Will. He simply carried on with his job on the dock as usual, kept himself to himself and did as he was told without raising any suspicion about his real purpose.

Because the office wasn't particularly busy, Richard took time off one morning to go riding with Joan. They dismounted at an animal track and began picking their way along it. The Yuletide would soon be upon them and this year Richard was providing the venison; he wanted to find the best spot to hunt for the deer when the time came.

When he spotted a young lad, he motioned Joan to stop and keep quiet. He left Diablo with her and crept off into the undergrowth. The poacher had fashioned a crude trap and was preparing to pull the twine which would drop the cage on top of the unsuspecting rabbit, but just as the culprit was about to snare his prey Richard caught him by the ear. The lad let out a scream of pain and the fortunate rabbit hopped off towards the safety of its burrow.

Richard led the young man by the ear back to where he had left Joan with the horses.

Surprised, Joan looked the urchin up and down. "Sam, is that really you?"

"I am so sorry, my lady, I didn't know this land belonged to you," he sobbed.

"This land belongs to me!" growled Richard. "But regardless of whose land it is, you were poaching!"

"Please, my lord, don't give me up to the authorities," Sam begged. "I didn't catch anything."

"Not for want of trying, you didn't," Richard retorted. "Give me one good reason why I shouldn't give you a good flogging and take you to the magistrate!"

"My Ma," Sam said. He dropped to his knees. "She'll die if I can't find food for her."

Joan lifted Sam from his knees. "Is your mother still sick, Sam? If I remember correctly the last time you were caught stealing you also got yourself into a lot of trouble. Did your head take long to heal?"

"Forgive me, but am I missing something here?" Richard put in. "Who is this boy, and how do you come to know who he is, Joan?"

Joan reminded her husband of when she was abducted by the smugglers and had been kept at the shepherd's hut. Sam had been forced to guard her there.

"This situation just gets worse," Richard said, on the verge of smiling. "Not only a poacher but a kidnapper to boot."

Terrified, Sam pleaded, "Please, sir, don't give me up! I'll do anything you ask but don't let them hang me!"

Richard arched an eyebrow. "Would that include doing a day's proper work to earn your bread instead of stealing?"

"I have no fear of work, my lord, but there is none to be had. And even if there was no-one would employ a wretch like me," Sam said tearfully.

"Well, Joan, what do you think?" Richard asked her. "Shall we take a chance and give this little thief some work, or should we pack him off to the authorities?"

"I will work as hard as I can every day and never steal from you, my lord," Sam promised, to which Richard replied, "Very wise, indeed. However, I am not 'my lord' but Sir Richard Lovell. I will be your master if you accept my offer of employment."

"Oh, yes, please, my lord. Sorry, Sir Richard, erm master?" Sam said, flustered. "You will never regret it, I promise!"

He kissed Joan's hand, and she laughed, "Very well, you young scamp but don't you dare let Sir Richard down or you might find yourself with another lump on the back of your head!"

"Do you know where my manor house is?" Richard asked him.

"Yes, sir."

"Good, then present yourself to my steward, Giles, an hour after dawn tomorrow, and don't be late."

With that settled, Richard and Joan turned and continued down the track. Sam raced off in the opposite direction as if the devil himself was chasing him.

When they reached the open road again, Joan gave Richard a huge hug and a long kiss. Smiling, Richard said, "That was very nice, but what was it for?"

"For being the most kind, caring man I know," Joan answered. "I am so proud to be your wife, my love! Thank you for giving Sam a chance to have a better life. I'm sure he won't let you down."

Happily, Sam proved to be both a willing worker and a quick learner. That he made a huge effort to carry out any task he was given, and the pleasant disposition with which he did so, soon endeared him to the rest of the manor staff. When a somewhat rundown cottage became available in the village closest to the manor, Sam and his mother were delighted to make it their own. Richard also gave Sam an advance, to allow the lad and his mother to buy the essentials they needed to live in their cottage comfortably.

With a proper roof over her head and regular food in her belly Sam's ma began to recover her health and soon was working with the other villagers. The physical exercise and better food equally benefitted Sam. He grew taller, his chest broadened, and he began to fill out; it soon became apparent he was leaving his boyhood behind and becoming a man. In his work with Barnaby, he learned how to take care of the horses and to repair and even make new tack for them. Henry showed him how to maintain Sir Richard's coach and how to drive it safely with the two horses. Sam was also responsible for ensuring the wood supply would keep the manor house fires burning, and he helped with any general maintenance on the estate. He more than lived up to the promise he gave to Richard that he would always work his hardest.

The Yule celebrations once again took place at Holyfield Hall. By now young Edmund was toddling competently; his antics kept everyone on their toes and he was thoroughly spoiled by both family and servants. Richard suggested he buy his son his first pony for Yuletide next year, until Joan gently reminded him that the child would only be two years and a few months old. They agreed it would be best to wait until Edmund was three years old—the same age they were when they were given their first ponies and taught to ride.

With the holidays over, life continued to roll along. Although Nicholas had no direct contact with Richard, he was always on the dock to receive his people when they arrived from the continent. It happened less often than Richard had feared, which eased his mind a little. The clandestine agent had told him that Walsingham's people had discovered quite a few more networks operating in other small ports. By spreading out the agents' arrival through the different ports, the foreign operatives raised little to no suspicion. Fortunately, they had no idea of Nicholas's betrayal and carried on with their mission in blissful ignorance, while Walsingham and his agents secretly gathered all the information needed to hang them and the converts to their cause.

Richard's new ship was more than half built, still on budget, and on schedule. He could hardly believe that in such a short space of time he had become the owner of three ocean going ships. Crew members from another ship recently returned from America told him that The Bonaventure and The Eleanor Joan had reached their destination safely. Richard was looking forward to their return in the spring with their holds full; he hoped nothing untoward would happen this time before they arrived back in England.

While Richard was at Holyfield, Edmund had asked his son to accompany him to survey both their estates, to determine where to site some new farmhouses. As Edmund owned far more land, it was decided that four large farms would be built on the Holyfield estate and two smaller ones on the manor estate. It was agreed that Edmund would oversee all the building work; he planned to begin building in early spring and hopefully start on the first crop sowing soon after. The project was a big gamble but Edmund's shrewd business sense had guided him well throughout his adult life. He hoped it would continue into his new venture.

Although Joan and Richard kept up their weekly lessons from Lorenzo, they worried less about needing to use their skills. Since Nicholas had returned, he'd steered clear of the manor and the office. Even though Richard still didn't trust the man he did feel slightly safer from his threats since he had become a double agent and was supposedly working for them now.

Richard's ships returned from the New World as soon as the weather allowed. They were caught by the tail end of a particularly nasty storm on the way, but thanks to the expert seamanship of Captain Ashe, closely followed by Captain Finch on The Eleanor Joan, both ships escaped any serious damage and kept their cargoes intact. Soon the courier arrived with a package from Hubert containing the money transfer order, along with a short note assuring Richard that his ships needed just a few minor repairs before they returned to America. Richard was relieved that the ships were sound but was even more relieved that he didn't have to go chasing off to London. Hubert had managed everything perfectly well on his own.

By the time Richard's ships returned from their next voyage they would find a sister ship waiting for them at the wharf. Ralph the shipbuilder had called in at the office just days ago to announce that work on the new ship should be completed within the month. Richard was delighted but struggled over what to call it. After much discussion he and Joan settled on The Edmund after Richard's father and their son. Edmund the elder was thrilled—but asked his son if the next one would be named 'The Richard' since the rest of the family now had ships carrying their name.

Richard laughed and proposed that they get

the current ship launched and off on her maiden voyage before they worried about a fourth.

During this time Joan had noticed that Giles was having mobility problems. His gait had become quite stiff and ungainly, and he seemed to be experiencing some pain when standing from a sitting position, or vice versa. These problems were brought home to Richard when Giles stumbled while carrying a tray of drinks, and a goblet of wine landed in his master's lap. Although Richard made light of the situation Giles was mortified—and even more so when it was suggested that he might find it easier to walk with the aid of a stick.

"What are we going to do about poor Giles?" Joan asked Richard. "He's obviously struggling but we can't just cast him out. He's been with me all my life and even when I was a child he seemed old. But now he really is getting old and frail. He has served my family well for his whole life and I won't reward that service by just dismissing him out of hand. He deserves to end his life in comfort and ease."

"I've no intention of casting him out, but I'm going to need a little time to come up with alternative arrangements," Richard answered. "When I let him go it will be with a small pension and a cottage to end his days in if he so wishes."

Joan thew her arms around his neck and kissed him. "I knew you wouldn't be unkind, my darling!

That's why I love you so very much."

The next morning Richard tracked Henry down at the stables, where he was with Sam working on one of the coach wheels. Henry was asked into the house where he was surprised to be shown into the family's inner sanctum and even more so when he was invited to sit.

"I don't suppose you know how to read and write do you, Henry?" Richard asked, more in hope than expectation.

"Yes, sir. I was taught to read and write as a child and then went on to the grammar school until I was fourteen."

"Is that so!" exclaimed Richard. "Then why on earth are you working as a coachman? Surely you are qualified to do so much more!"

The expression on the man's face, a mixture of sadness and shame, made Richard quickly apologize, "I'm sorry, Henry. That is none of my business. I spoke out of turn."

"No, sir, I believe you are entitled to know why you have an educated coachman," Henry answered. He took a deep breath before he continued, "I was apprenticed to a man who scribed for anyone who needed documents prepared or letters written. He had no heir, just one daughter, Isobel. I loved my job there, sir, and the man I worked for, but certainly not Isobel. She set her cap at me but I didn't nor ever could love her. She was not a nice person. Whenever I was alone she was there making improper suggestions and trying to kiss me. I wasn't interested and so she attempted to trap me into a marriage by running to her father and telling him I had compromised her."

Henry gave Richard an imploring look. "Believe me, sir, I hadn't touched her. I didn't even like her. I think her father just wanted rid of her to any man. When he challenged me about my supposed behaviour, he offered to leave me everything in his will including his business if I would marry Isobel. I refused and said I would rather be out on the street before I would allow myself to be shackled to his daughter. By the end of the day that is exactly where I was, sir, on the street with no employment, no home and no prospects. The man I had so looked up to was very well known and liked in the town and made it quite clear that he would let everyone know what a low-life character I was and how I'd led his daughter on. There was no future for me there, so I made my way to Topsham not knowing what I was going to do. Fortunately, I arrived just at the time you were looking for a coachman."

When Richard frowned, Henry said, "I'm sorry I wasn't entirely straight with you, sir. If you are going to dismiss me I will understand."

"What? No of course I'm not going to dismiss you!" Richard returned. "On the contrary you have been a very diligent member of my staff, and if you are willing, I would like to offer you a substantial promotion."

Confused, Henry asked, "What sort of promotion?"

"To that of my steward," Richard said.

Henry stared at Richard.

"Well?" Richard prompted. "Are you going to give me your answer?"

"I'm finding it hard to take in, sir. I'm not sure I'm worthy to be your steward. It's the highest position in your household."

"Let me be the judge of that, Henry. I would like you to work along with Giles for a while and learn what will be required of you. When he is satisfied that you are ready to take over, that will be good enough for me. Are you willing?"

"Yes, Sir Richard, I am willing and deeply thankful for the opportunity," Henry replied. "I just hope that I'm not a disappointment to you."

"I'll be a very surprised man if you are."

Richard stood and offered his hand to Henry. They shook hands with enthusiasm.

After Richard had left Henry with Giles, he headed back to the stables. Sam was still there, looking at the carriage wheel. "Is it ready to go back on?" Richard asked him.

When Sam nodded, Richard said, "Very well then, I'll give you a hand."

By the time the wheel had been replaced both men were breathing heavily. "Do you have any small ale here?" Richard asked. Sam ran into the stables and reappeared with a jug of small ale and two wooden cups. Over their drinks Richard gave

Sam the news that he was now the new coachman. Sam was thrilled, both with the promotion and the pay increase. Richard told him to take Henry's uniform up to the house where Agnes would do any necessary alterations.

Barnaby and Joan returned from their ride rosy-cheeked and out of breath. When Richard told Joan about his morning's work, she wholeheartedly approved and was pleased that Giles's well-deserved retirement was now in sight. She was thrilled for Sam, too. He had proved his worth many times over.

Captain Ashe arrived a few days later to personally give Richard his report. Richard's crews had taken both ships to a nearby shipyard, before they left for their shore leave, where all the visible repairs were to be made, as well as a thorough check below the waterline. Otherwise, it had been another successful and lucrative crossing. The two men discussed building a wharf big enough to take all the ships for the loading and unloading of their cargoes. It would save a great deal of time and energy loading straight onto the ships, instead of having to ferry everything back and forth in small boats. Richard thought it something well worth considering especially as timber was so cheap in the New World. He promised Tom he would look into it. He also asked Tom to start thinking about a crew and captain for the new ship.

Nodding, Tom said, "Whenever I'm in port I

get numerous inquiries from sailors wishing to sign on but the crews already manning your ships are keen to stay where they are, sir. They are well paid and get handsome bonuses and that doesn't go unnoticed."

"That may be so but those men have to work hard for those wages and bonuses and not only aboard ship, Tom. On land in America they become builders as well as other things, as you well know. It will be my sailors who will build the wharves with a little professional guidance if I decide to go ahead with the plan," Richard said. "Any man you take on must be made aware of what will be expected of him and if there's any doubt you must not even consider him."

"Never fear, sir. I will be sure before I sign any man on here or in London."

"Will you find sailors here, Tom?"

"I'm sure I will, sir," Tom answered. "Probably a few who are already serving on your smaller ships as well as good men looking for work. As any work is very hard to come by, I'm sure I'll be able to put a capable crew together for the ship's maiden voyage."

"What about a captain?" Richard asked him. "That might not be so easy. If they already have a ship, they're not likely to be interested in leaving it—and if they don't it's probably because they're second rate. I only want the best."

"I think I know where to find him, sir, but if he accepts you'll be a captain short on one of your smaller ships."

"Go on," urged Richard.

"Before I settled on Captain Finch for The Eleanor Joan, I was considering Captain Matthew Kytson. He's a first-class sailor and runs a tight ship but is fair and his men know it. He is well respected by his crew and is as honest as the day is long. I would have no hesitation in offering him the job."

Richard nodded. "I know him and I like what I have seen. He's a good man and hasn't put a foot wrong in all the years I've known him. I think he's an excellent choice. When you arrange to speak to him, I would like to be there too."

"Here in your office, sir?"

"Perfect! I'll leave you to organise the interview then." Richard stood and held out his hand to his captain. "It's been really good to see you again Tom. Let's get this business over quickly and then you can get off on your shore leave."

As luck would have it, Captain Kytson was at sea. It was another two weeks before Tom brought him to Richard's office.

"Do you know why you are here, Captain Kytson?" Richard asked him.

"Not really, sir. Tom told me you both needed to speak to me. I hope I've done nothing wrong."

"Absolutely not, Matthew!" Richard reassured him. He nodded to Tom, who quickly explained the situation. When Tom asked him if would be willing to accept, Matthew readily replied, "If you are sure, sir, then I would be honoured."

"Good!" Richard answered, smiling. "Let us go to the shipyard where you can meet your new ship and become acquainted with her. She will be ready to put to sea by the end of the month and you and your new crew will sail her down to London to join my other two ships."

Ralph was pleased to see Richard, and Richard was delighted to hear that his new ship would be handed over to him by the end of the week. Everything was progressing quicker than expected; Tom even had enough crew to get her to London. The last few could be signed on there.

All of the family attended the naming ceremony, but none were as proud as Edmund. The ship set sail immediately after the ceremony and there were tears in Edmunds eyes as his namesake slipped her moorings and headed off down the river.

Richard was a happy man. All being well, soon his three ships would be leaving for America and hopefully all with full holds.

Richard hadn't spoken to Nicholas since he first returned from London as a double agent, and Walsingham's man hadn't made any unannounced visits in the middle of the night for some time. Could it be that at last Richard was getting his life back on an even keel? The changes he'd made at home had worked out well. Henry was getting on with Giles and taking over bit by bit; a cottage was ready for the old steward for when he finally retired; and Sam was now the proud owner of a good pair of leggings, a heavy jacket, a pair of fine leather boots, a cloak and hat that he wore when he drove the coach.

Family life was happy, too. Little Edmund was growing into quite a little character. His favourite game was for his papa to chase him up the garden path, grab him, throw up in the air, and catch him on the way down. As soon as Edmund was on the ground again he would take off along the path as fast as his chubby little legs would carry him.

And then, of course, Richard had Joan. He couldn't have felt more satisfied.

One morning he and William were working their way through the paperwork on their respective desks when the door opened. Richard carried on reading a document, until a commanding voice said, "Sir Richard Lovell, I'm arresting you on the charge of treason!"

Richard's head snapped up.

He found himself staring into the eyes of a local constable, accompanied by two soldiers—one of whom had the point of his sword at Will's throat.

"On whose authority?" Richard protested jumping up from his stool. "I'm no more a traitor than you are!"

"I'm sorry, Sir Richard, but a claim has been made that you have been using your ships to smuggle illegal persons into England from the continent," the constable told him. "It must be assumed that these foreigners are spies or people sent to disturb Her Majesty's peace. Either way, it is a treasonable offence. I'm afraid you must come with me, sir. I have orders to deliver you to the Justice in Exeter immediately."

"There must be some mistake!" Richard argued. "This is ridiculous! What about my wife and family? Am I not even allowed to see them before you drag me off?"

"My orders say immediately, sir," the constable replied. He nodded towards the soldier standing beside him. When the soldier fettered Richard's hands and feet with the chains, Richard snapped, "My God! Is this really necessary?"

"I'm afraid it is. Treason is the most serious of charges, and I cannot risk the chance that given the opportunity you might try to escape."

"At least let me have my cloak," Richard returned. "The weather is still quite cold."

"Very well! You fetch his cloak," the constable growled at Will.

Terrified, Will lifted the cloak from its peg and flung it round Richard's shoulders. As he was fastening the clasp Richard whispered in his ear, "Tell Joan to get a message to Walsingham as soon as she can."

With that the three men hustled Richard out of his office and down the dock to the waiting cart. When they'd gone, Will ran for the stables at The Bush as fast as his legs would carry him. In no time he was on the way to the manor and Joan with the terrible news, Diablo in tow.

•

# CHAPTER 9

When Will charged into the parlour shortly thereafter, Joan jumped up from her chair, dropping her needlework onto the floor—only to collapse back into her chair after she heard that Richard had been arrested for treason, and was already on his way to Exeter in chains. She grasped the arms of her chair and forced herself to take deep breaths. When she had calmed herself enough to speak, she said, "There must be a mistake Will! Who arrested him?"

"A constable arrived with two soldiers. He said he had orders to take Richard to the Justice in Exeter. There was nothing I could do, Joan. One of the soldiers had his sword pointed at my throat. I couldn't even leave my desk."

"What about my husband?" she asked. "What did Richard say?"

"He denied being a traitor, of course, but other than that he could do nothing. The constable had a document, signed by the Justice, authorising Richard's arrest."

"Oh my God, Will. What are we to do?" Joan

despaired. "It must be a mistake! Maybe they have arrested the wrong man!"

"I'm sorry, Joan, but there was no mistake."

Joan leapt from her chair. "I must speak to Barnaby!" she declared. She ran for the door leaving Will staring after her.

She arrived at the stables so out of breath that her groom forced her to sit on one of the benches nearby until she regained her composure. He had already guessed that something was amiss when Will had galloped into the yard and ran for the house, leaving both his horse and Diablo to wander about the yard unattended. In garbled words which Barnaby found hard to follow Joan explained Richard's predicament. She concluded with, "You must ride to Holyfield at once and bring Lord Edmund back with you. He will know what to do! You must hurry, Barnaby—anything could be happening to Sir Richard!"

When she returned to the parlour, she found Will sitting with his head in his hands. "Don't worry," Joan told him. "Lord Edmund will soon sort this mess out."

At least she fervently hoped that he would.

A few hours later Barnaby returned with Lord and Lady Lovell. When Richard's parents entered the parlour, they found Joan pacing up and down, and poor Will trying to calm her, without much success.

Joan embraced first Edmund and then Eleanor before Edmund asked Will to relate again exactly what had transpired in the office. When Will finished Edmund announced that he would leave for Exeter early the following morning to seek out the Justice and discover just what evidence had led to Richard's arrest.

Joan was still awake when the first light of day crept through the shutters. She had spent the entire night imagining what horrific things might happen to her beloved if he was found guilty. Surely they wouldn't convict an innocent man? But she knew from her time at the Queen's court that these things did happen, and more frequently than most people would imagine. She also knew the bloodcurdling details of a traitor's death. She shuddered as she pulled the bedcovers tighter and began to weep softly.

Eleanor stayed with Joan at the manor while Edmund made his trip to Exeter and Will went to work at the office in Topsham. Waiting for Edmund to return was the longest day of Joan's life. Even a visit from baby Edmund failed to lift her spirits. Eleanor was in the same state and the two women spent the time trying to reassure each other that all would be well, but the expression on Edmund's face when he returned was enough to let them know that everything was definitely not well. He dropped down heavily onto the nearest chair, looking tired and defeated.

"When I arrived, I spent over an hour waiting for the Justice to see me," he told them. "When I was eventually shown into his office, I recognised the man. He is Sir Edward Radcliffe, a well-respected man known for his fair and balanced judgement. We are acquaintances only but have met on the odd occasion when we were attending the same function. He told me that the evidence against Richard is overwhelming. Apparently, half a dozen sailors from different crews have come forward and are willing to testify that they had been ordered to accept unknown persons as crew members on numerous occasions, and that these unknown persons were ferried covertly from the continent to Topsham. The captain of one of those ships will also give evidence that Sir Richard directed that anyone who presented the password 'Willum' was to be allowed on board with no questions asked. It isn't looking good, especially as Richard is refusing to put up a defence against these charges."

"But why?" Eleanor demanded. "What's wrong with the boy? Doesn't he realise his life is at stake?"

"Surely if this Sir Edward is as fair as you say father, we can explain that this is all a mistake and he will release Richard?" Joan put in.

Edmund shook his head. "I'm afraid not, Joan. It is out of his hands. He can only try certain crimes as a Justice. A person charged with treason must be tried by the Queen's Commissioner at the Quarter Sessions. The next one is due in Exeter in a fortnight's time. Richard has until then to come up with his defence."

Joan began to weep again. "Where is he, Father? Did you see him?"

"I wasn't allowed to see him, but he is not being held in the dungeon. He is being kept in one of the better cells above ground and, before I started for home, I left money with Sir Edward for Richard to be fed with decent food while he's there."

"Will I be able to see him?" she asked tearfully.

"I'm afraid not, my dear. He's not to be allowed any visitors at all before his trial."

Tears gave way to anger, as Joan exclaimed, "Oh, poor Richard, he'll be all alone and frightened with no-one to talk to. It's all so unfair! We all know that he's not a traitor. He could never be a traitor."

"Surely Walsingham could do something to stop this," Eleanor stated crossly.

"I've already sent a message to Walsingham," Joan told her. "Will was to leave the letter at The Bush on his way to the office. Sir Francis's agent should forward it."

Sounding sceptical, Eleanor asked, "How long will it take to reach him, and how much longer until we get a reply?"

"His network will get the message there and back in time as long as Walsingham is in London when it arrives."

"Even then there's no guarantee that the man will lift a finger to help Richard," Edmund said sombrely. "That will be why Richard has no defence. It would be his word against Walsingham and he knows that the man wouldn't risk his entire venture for one man's life--even his Walsingham would deny all knowledge."

A dark mood had settled over the parlour by the time Will arrived home. He confirmed that he had left Joan's message at The Bush, with instructions that it was to be delivered to Walsingham as a matter of urgency. Now all the family could do was hope.

Richard paced around his small cell for the umpteenth time before he stopped and stared out at the wall opposite through the barred window. He was still trying to come to terms with his situation. Yesterday had started as a normal working day and finished with him locked in a cell, charged with treason. When he'd arrived in Exeter he was taken to appear in front of the Justice. His shackles were removed and he'd been allowed to sit. One soldier stood inside the door and the other on guard outside while the constable gave his report.

The Justice introduced himself as Sir Edward Radcliffe. Richard noted that he was a man of small stature who managed to portray a much larger presence. His eyes were shrewd and piercing, and spectacles were perched on his long, straight nose. His thin face and lips were almost lost behind his still full beard although the greying hair on his head was less so. Richard guessed that the man was in his late forties or even older, and when he spoke it was with a voice of authority.

"Sir Richard, I must admit that when this charge was brought against you, I was very surprised," Sir Edward told him. "I have met your father occasionally over the years when our paths have crossed and was very impressed by the way he conducted himself. He struck me as a very upright and honest person. He together with his Guild have done great things for Exeter, not least the grammar school. He is a man worthy of respect. I have also taken the time to investigate your reputation, too, and have found nothing that would lead me to believe you capable of the crime for which you have been charged. You are spoken of fondly as following in your father's footsteps as a fair, honest and upstanding man. The evidence against you is overwhelming," Sir Edward continued, "but I am hoping that you will present a robust defence, strong enough to persuade the jury that the claims are not what they seem, and to return a not guilty verdict."

Richard lifted his chin. "No defence!"

"You must understand that on the evidence already presented against you, and without any defence, the jury will find you guilty and you will be sentenced to death," the Justice warned him. "Will you not reconsider?"

"No defence," repeated Richard.

"Very well. You will be kept confined in your cell until the Queen's Commissioner arrives in two weeks. I hope you will use that time to rethink your decision to present no defence. At that time the law will follow its course to its conclusion and there will be nothing I can do to help you."

Richard thanked Sir Edward for his concern, and asked if he would allow him to write a note to his wife. Permission was granted with the proviso that the authorities would read the letter before it was delivered. Richard agreed, thanked the Justice again and was led to his cell.

In the morning a guard entered his prison with parchment, quill and ink and placed it all on the small table. "Compliments of the Justice, but why a traitor should be given such preferential treatment is beyond me!" the guard grumbled.

"I haven't yet been tried let alone found guilty of treason and condemned." Richard retorted.

"Oh, you will be, Sir Richard, never you fear," countered the man before he left, carefully locking the door behind him.

Richard sat down at the table and visualised Joan's beautiful face. He picked up the quill, dipped it in the ink and began to write.

My darling wife, I am well and reasonably comfortable in this place, but I am missing you dreadfully already. Did you manage to complete the task that Will set you? I hope so. I am so sorry that this has happened, mostly because I know what it will be doing to you, my love. Give young Edmund a kiss from his papa as I send my love to you. Try not to worry about me too much. Pray for me as I do for you and our son. Take heed when you reply as your letter will be read by the authorities before I receive it. Always remember you are my world. Yours now and forever, Richard.

He folded the parchment and kissed it tenderly before he placed it back on the table. An hour later a young man entered his cell, followed by the guard. He collected the letter and promised to deliver it to Topsham. Richard lay on his cot and stared at the ceiling. Now what the hell was he going to do for two weeks? The delay would prolong the agony. If he told the Justice that no other than Sir Francis Walsingham had ordered him to ship these foreigners into the country secretly the man would laugh in his face. If by any chance Sir Edward did believe him, what then? Would Walsingham hold his hands up and admit it? Highly unlikely. The operation to trap and capture the agents and their accomplices was huge and nationwide. Walsingham would never put all that at risk just to save one man's life. Richard was doomed to die for a crime he hadn't committed.

Or had he? After all, it was by his orders that the agents were smuggled into the country illegally. What a bloody mess he had got into. As far as he could see there was no way out.

He turned onto his side, faced the wall and let the tears flow, not for himself but for Joan. Once again she would be tainted by treason through no fault of her own. What kind of life would he leave for his wife and son once he'd been executed? Yes, his parents would love and protect them for as long as they were alive, but then what? Who would care for them after his mother and father had departed this world? Would his beloved Joan remarry? The very thought of her giving herself to another man broke his heart.

Damn Walsingham! Damn him to hell!

Three very long and agonising days went by before he received Joan's reply.

My dearest Richard, I love and miss you too, very much, as does baby Edmund. Yes, I did complete Will's task. I can hardly bear being without you. You must defend yourself, my love, or all will be lost. Don't leave me and Edmund all alone! Defend yourself! Please my darling. Your parents send their love. We need you home again. We are all praying for you. I love you with all my heart. Your Joan.

The letter was still legible but had smears where her tears had fallen onto her words. He held it to his chest as he imagined holding her in his arms. He remembered how she would snuggle down to sleep at night with her head on his shoulder and her arm draped over his stomach. Choking back his tears, Richard sniffed the perfume on her letter once again before he folded it and put it in his pocket. He knew that he had already held Joan for the last time, and that for what was left of his life he would be sleeping alone in a miserable cell.

Once again he despaired over how he could possibly defend himself. Walsingham would never back his claim. He would be looked on as a cowardly cur attempting to save his own skin by implicating the very man who protected the nation and the Queen from all outside threats. He would be branded a fool and a liar as well as a traitor. He didn't want to leave that legacy for his son. It would be hard enough for the boy. No! When the time came, he would die bravely with his head held high—although when he thought of what a traitor's death entailed, he visibly paled. May God help him if it came to that.

It was late on in the day before his trial when he received a visit from the Queen's Commissioner. The opulently dressed man swaggered into the cell, sat his over-sized body down on the only chair and glared at Richard. Richard in turn stood and stared back at the man. He was almost Richard's height but obese. His fat ruddy cheeks almost obscured his little piglike eyes, and his large fleshy lips forced their way between his black beard and moustache.

Neither man was inclined to drop his gaze but it was the Commissioner who spoke first. "I am Lord William Ridley, Her Majesty the Queen's Commissioner, and I will be presiding over your trial tomorrow. I have saved your trial for last as I like to end my quarterly visits with at least one hanging. This time it will be a traitor's death—quite a spectacle."

"I think you might have overlooked something," Richard returned. "I haven't even had my trial yet so how can you be so certain about the sentence?"

"Because I have read the evidence against you and because Radcliffe tells me you aren't putting up a defence. The jury will certainly return a guilty verdict, giving me the pleasure of passing the death sentence. Death by hanging, drawing and quartering. The people are already gathering to witness your end, Lovell, and many more will be there tomorrow. When it is done the crowd will remember it for years to come and I will leave this place a happy man. Until tomorrow!"

Lord Ridley rose and left the cell laughing. Richard knew then that his fate was sealed. He threw himself onto his cot, closed his eyes and imagined his beautiful Joan lying beside him for one last time, at least in this world.

The time for his trial arrived. A jury of his peers sat in their places. The prosecutor was also present, and the Justice positioned beside the Queen's Commissioner at a large table. All that was missing was the accused.

Richard was escorted in fetters from his cell by six soldiers. Their route deliberately took them past the gallows; the sight of it made Richard swallow hard. There were a couple of jeers as he passed through the large crowd, but apart from some women sobbing the large gathering was silent. This behaviour unnerved the solders as they were used to the populace baying for the prisoner's blood.

His escort tried to hurry Richard along but the chains around his ankles made that impossible. His walk of shame was made a little easier thanks to Joan, who had sent his shaving kit and clean clothes, ensuring he was at least neatly shaven and tidily dressed. After he'd made himself presentable Richard had been visited in his cell by a minister and given time to make his peace with God.

The courtroom was silent, apart from the jangling of his chains. He heard a sharp intake of breath from the front row of the public gallery where he saw Joan sitting with his parents. She could not take her eyes off her husband, who looked so haggard and tired. Eleanor began to sob quietly while Edmund gripped her hand as he stared at his son, unable to believe that this was really happening. Richard glanced at them and gave them a weak smile before facing the Commissioner.

The Commissioner called the court to order. He read out the charges against Richard, and asked how Richard pleaded, but received no response. He repeated his question; when Richard still remained silent he told him to sit down. The prosecutor then proceeded to call his witnesses one after the other to give their testimony. Not one of the men looked at Richard while giving his evidence. Upon the conclusion of each man's testimony, Richard was asked if he had any questions. Each time he shook his head and quietly said, "No questions." He saw no use in questioning the seamen. They were only telling the truth of what they had seen.

When the captain had given his evidence there were a few murmurings from the members of the public. What was wrong with Sir Richard? Why wouldn't he defend himself? Didn't he understand that he was on trial for his life? The jury also showed some signs of confusion. With a malicious smile, the Commissioner called for silence before he asked the prisoner to reply to the accusations made against him.

Richard stood up and said in a clear, firm voice, "I have no defence, sir."

Joan leapt out of her seat. "No!" she exclaimed. "Say something Richard! Defend yourself!"

The Commissioner hit the desk with his gavel. "If you interrupt this court again, I will have you removed," he bellowed.

Edmund gently helped Joan back into her seat. Richard knew she must be distraught, but there was nothing he could do to ease her pain.

"Sir Richard Lovell," the Commissioner boomed, "do you have anything at all that you wish to say?"

"No, my lord."

With a vindictive smile the Commissioner passed the case over to the jury and charged them to return a verdict. The evidence was so overwhelming and undisputed that their deliberation was soon completed. "Have you reached your verdict?" Lord William asked them eagerly.

"We have, my lord. We find the prisoner guilty of the charge of treason."

Joan jumped to her feet again "He isn't a traitor! He's innocent! You are making a big mistake!"

"I won't warn you again!" the Commissioner snapped. "Sit down!"

Edmund dragged Joan down to her seat and held both her and Eleanor's hands as they awaited the pronouncement.

With obvious relish the Commissioner said to Richard, "You will be taken from here to the place of your execution, where you will be hanged, drawn and quartered. May God have mercy on your soul."

Richard's legs threatened to give way under him.

"He's innocent!" screamed Joan. "He's not a traitor!"

It made no difference. The soldiers had already begun to lead Richard away to his death. He glanced at his family once more before he was hustled through the door, his eyes full of sadness.

The huge crowd was silent as the small party made their way to the scaffold where the minister and the executioner waited. The Commissioner was somewhat unnerved by the peoples' behaviour. Why were they not in the normal celebratory mood when a traitor was about to die? An execution was usually a time of great merriment for the mob. He moved a little closer to the soldiers.

As Richard slowly climbed the steps of the scaffold he noticed the fire where his entrails would be burnt in front of him while he was still alive. When he looked up he saw the noose, which would hang him until he was almost dead. He reached the top of the steps where he knelt before the minister. He prayed that God would give him the strength to bear this ordeal and when it was over to accept his miserable soul and watch over Joan and baby Edmund.

Despite Edmund's best efforts to persuade the ladies to remain in the courtroom, Joan declared that she would not let Richard die alone, and Eleanor insisted that her son would need his mother's presence now more than ever. The crowd respectfully parted to let the small family take up position in front of the platform where Richard was about give up his life.

His fetters were removed and his hands tied behind him. The executioner knelt before him to ask forgiveness for what he was about to do, as was the custom. Richard readily forgave him and once again faced the people, many of whom were openly sobbing. His eyes soon rested on his beloved Joan's face and he gave her the broadest of smiles. He mouthed the words, "I love you," just as the Commissioner shouted, "Sir Richard Lovell, you have been found guilty of treason in a court of law and as the law decrees you will suffer a traitor's death. You will be hanged and cut down while you still breathe, your entrails will be removed and burnt in front of your eyes while you still live, your heart will be ripped out and your head removed before your body is quartered."

Edmund laboured to support Joan and Eleanor, both of whom now wilted in despair. There were shouts of *No!* from various sections of the crowd.

Lord Ridley looked about nervously. He was beginning to fear that the people might try to release Richard. "Get on with the execution, you fool!" he hissed.

The executioner put the noose over Richard's head and tightened it. He motioned Richard to climb the ladder resting on the crossbeam of the scaffold. The executioner then pulled the rope almost taut and tied it securely. He turned and kicked the ladder away, leaving Richard hanging in mid-air.

Richard threw his legs about wildly as some in the crowd began to boo. Joan fainted when her husband lost consciousness, while Eleanor lamented, "Oh my poor boy, my poor boy." Even Edmund sobbed uncontrollably.

The Commissioner, on the other hand, watched Richard's agony with a smug smile.

The executioner cut the prisoner down and laid him on his back for the next stage in the gruesome procedure. However, Richard needed to be conscious before the executioner could begin.

There was a commotion at the edge of the

gathering as a rider tried to force his way through the throng. "Make way!" he shouted. "Stop the execution in the name of the Queen! Make way!"

The crowd quickly parted and let the rider and his exhausted horse through to the scaffold. Edmund and Eleanor, who were both trying to support Joan's sagging body, desperately tried to see what was going on.

"Who the hell are you? This is a legal execution!" the Commissioner raged. "The prisoner has been tried, found guilty and sentenced. It cannot be stopped!" He turned toward the executioner. "Get on with it!"

The executioner removed his knife from his belt and cut through Richard's shirt, exposing his chest, and then made to slice through the top of his leggings.

"Hold!" shouted the messenger. "If you go ahead with this you will be committing murder!"

The executioner looked at the Commissioner and the rider in turn, not knowing what to do.

The rider waved a pouch in front of Lord William. "You need to read this before you go any further. It contains a letter from Her Majesty the Queen!"

Lord William took the pouch with ill grace and opened the letter. Elizabeth herself had signed it. As much as he wanted to bring the execution to its grisly conclusion, he knew that if he disobeyed a direct order from his sovereign, he would soon find himself in the same position as Richard. The frustrated man slapped the document onto the Justice's chest and stormed off angrily pushing his way through the inquisitive crowd.

As the Justice read the letter, he smiled to himself. "The verdict and the sentence in the case of Sir Richard Lovell have been quashed by order of Her Majesty the Queen," he declared loudly, and the crowd erupted into cheers. He instructed the soldiers to take the prisoner back to his cell and to send for the physician to tend him. The Justice then walked over to Richard's family, now weeping not in terror but with relief. "I would like you come with me, please," he said. "There is something you must see."

Sir Edward led them to his office and spread the Queen's order out on his desk. "This missive explains that Sir Richard was part of a secret mission instigated by Her Majesty," he said, "and although all the evidence pointed to treason, it was part of a bigger plan to rid the realm of hundreds of traitors, which was sanctioned by the Queen herself. Sir Richard is to be released with all charges against him dropped, and he is to be given any assistance he requires from the judiciary both now and in the future. The document has been signed by Queen Elizabeth herself."

Sir Edward shook his head. "Why didn't he speak up at the beginning? Surely he must have realised that he would be found guilty and executed."

"Because he knew as soon as he was charged

with treason that his life was forfeit. The scheme he was involved in has to succeed and he would not betray his sovereign or his country even if it cost him his life," Edmund replied.

"Dear God, we almost executed a true patriot who was working for the good of the realm, not against it!" said the horrified Justice. "Thank God the messenger arrived in time!"

"Thank God indeed!" echoed Edmund. "Although it was a close-run thing."

"On the evidence presented, and the fact that Richard refused to defend himself, the verdict would always have been guilty and rightly so," said Sir Edward. "However, the way the Commissioner conducted the trial was most unprofessional, and his vindictive behaviour reprehensible. I will be sending a full report to my superiors even if it might lead to me losing my own position as Justice. These men tend to defend each other."

"If you need any corroboration of the facts, I would be happy to add my name," Edmund told him.

"Thank you, Lord Lovell, you are most kind."

Caught between relief and desperation, Joan asked, "Can I see my husband now?"

"Of course, my lady," Sir Edward answered. "I will escort you myself."

Eleanor rose to follow but Edmund held her back. "We will see him later, my love," he assured her. "They need some time together, just the two of them. It has been a traumatic time for us all but imagine what it must have been like for Richard and Joan."

Eleanor nodded and sat down again beside her husband. She would see her son soon.

When Richard opened his eyes, he couldn't understand why he was back in his cell, nor did he recognise the man standing over him. He tried to speak but couldn't form any words; his throat was on fire. When he began to cough, the stranger sent a soldier to get him something to drink. The unknown man then introduced himself as a physician and dismissed the remaining soldiers.

The physician examined Richard's neck and throat. He winced whenever the man touched a particularly tender spot.

"I can't see any obvious damage to your throat," the physician said, "so I'm hoping you will suffer no permanent injury. Your voice should return in time but I must warn you that it may be a different timbre to what it used to be. Your neck will be sore for some time, as well. It has severe rope burns and is badly bruised. When it has healed you will probably be left with some scarring. On the whole I think you have been very fortunate."

Richard wanted to tell the man just how fortunate he felt after being half hanged for something he didn't do, but it was hopeless. He couldn't speak.

The soldier returned carrying a tankard of

ale. The feeling had returned to Richards hands, although there was still a nasty welt around his wrists. He sat up, swung his legs over the side of his cot, and eagerly accepted the tankard from the soldier. When he took a long swig, most of the mouthful ended up running down his chest, because he couldn't swallow. It was only then that he noticed his slashed shirt and he realised with a jolt just how close to his death he had been.

"Slowly, slowly Richard. Just a sip at a time," advised the physician. Indeed, it took several attempts before he could swallow without choking. By the time the tankard was empty there was far more ale on him and the floor than down his throat.

The physician patted his shoulder. "You won't be surprised to hear that it will also be a while before you can manage solid food again. However, I'm sure your wife will be able to cope with that problem."

At this mention of Joan, she appeared with the Justice. The physician and the Justice withdrew, leaving the cell door ajar. When Richard raised pained blue eyes to her, she ran to him and flung her arms around his neck, only to jump back when he cried out. It was then that she saw just how sore and bruised his neck was.

"Oh, my love, I am so sorry!" she exclaimed. "Is it terribly sore?"

Richard nodded.

She pushed his hair back from his face and

kissed him tenderly. "I was sure I was going to lose you, my darling," she whispered. "It was too much to bear. How did you manage to be so brave?"

Richard shrugged his shoulders and gave her a silly lopsided grin.

"Haven't you got anything to say?" she asked him.

Richard pointed to his mouth and shook his head. When Joan realised that he couldn't speak, she began to cry, but stopped after Richard put his finger to her lips and shook his head. She wiped her eyes with the back of her hand, and they embraced and kissed each other. When they separated Richard began to look around the cell.

"What's the matter, my love?" she asked him. "What are you looking for?"

Richard took her hand and placed it on his bare chest and shuddered.

"You're cold!" Joan said.

He smiled and mimed throwing his cloak around his shoulders.

They found it on the floor, between the cot and the wall. Joan quickly fastened it around his shoulders before Richard pulled her close and kissed her again. This was how Edmund and Eleanor found them when they entered the cell. Joan pointed out the injuries on Richard's neck and explained that he couldn't speak at the moment, upon which Edmund gave his son a big hug. "I thought I had lost you," he said. "Why did you not defend yourself?"

Richard looked at his father and raised his eyebrows.

"Oh, you silly old man!" Eleanor admonished Edmund. "How can he answer you when he can't talk?" She took her beloved son in her arms and whispered in his ear, "Don't think you won't have to explain yourself once you can talk again!"

Richard returned her hug and kissed the top of her head.

There was a tap on the door and the Justice entered, holding some documents. "These are your papers, Richard," he said. "They exonerate you from all the charges. You are free to go. Please accept my sincere apologies."

Richard grasped the man's proffered hand; the expression in his eyes conveyed that he held no ill will toward the Justice.

Joan slipped her hand through Richard's arm and addressed Sir Edward, "Can we go home now?"

"Of course. I'll escort you to your coach."

Sam had been kicking his heels for some time now. When he saw his master walking towards him, he smiled from one side of his face to the other. Richard reached out and squeezed the boy's shoulder.

"Take us home, Sam," Edmund said, laughing, "but do take care. We've had enough drama for one day."

# CHAPTER 10

It was an uneventful journey home from Exeter. Richard, emotionally and physically drained, slept for most of it. The rest of the family felt a great sense of relief, now that the most unbearable of burdens had been lifted from their shoulders. They had come so close to losing Richard, thanks to Walsingham and his grand plan.

When they arrived at the manor the coach hurtled through the gate without slowing and carried on until it reached the steps in front of the house. The staff filed out and stood in line on the steps, ready to greet the grieving family believing that their young master had not only been executed but would also have been denied a proper burial and grave.

First to alight was Lord Edmund. He helped Lady Joan and then Lady Eleanor step down from the coach. The staff looked on in tears, or very close to it, but when Sir Richard appeared, their elation was palpable. Maisie the cook was so overcome with happiness that she ran up to the master and gave him a huge hug before falling back in a fluster and apologising for her presumption. Richard tried to laugh and returned the hug.

Over the din of everyone talking at once Edmund promised that after the family had recovered from their journey home, they would explain everything. Giles quickly dispersed the staff but not before Eleanor had a private word with Maisie. Joan sent Agnes to the nursery to instruct Mary to bring the baby to the parlour where a welcoming fire was burning in the grate.

Joan, Eleanor and Edmund sat down to await their refreshments and young Edmund, but Richard walked about the room, running his hand over the backs of the chairs and across the table. He picked up a book he had been reading before he'd been arrested, glanced through a couple of pages and put it down again. He stood looking out of the window at the beautiful view of the garden. Joan walked to his side and reached for his hand, noticing that his eyes were wet with tears.

"You didn't think you'd ever see home again, did you, my love," she whispered.

He shook his head, still looking out over the garden.

"You're safe now," Joan told him. "You have been pardoned by the Queen herself and no-one dare hurt you– not even Walsingham. We are free at last."

Richard turned towards her. He took her other hand in his, kissed her forehead, the tip of her nose and finally her lips before taking her into his arms.

They were still standing at the window when Mary came into the room with little Edmund toddling beside her, holding onto her hand. When he saw his mama and papa he pulled his hand free and hurried to Richard, who already had his arms open and ready to catch him. He swung his son up to his chest and hugged him tightly while making grunting noises in his throat. Little Edmund thought that this was all part of a game and chuckled as he tried to put his fingers into Richard's mouth.

A happy half hour was spent by the family. Edmund entertained them with his antics as he ran from one to the other demanding their attention. Mary whispered to Joan when it was time for the baby to be fed and put to bed for the night. Goodnights were said to the little man but his noisy protests at being removed from the parlour could be heard long after he had left the room.

By the time Will returned after a miserable day at the office, Richard had poured the wine and everyone had settled around the fire again. Dreading what he would find at the house, Will had dismounted at the stable, only to be surprised by Sam appearing, smiling broadly. He soon conveyed the good news about Richard's acquittal to Will who ran to the house to see with his own eyes that his friend had indeed been spared.

They were all talking excitedly when Agnes

and Ellen arrived with bowls of boiled and cooled water, fresh dressings and a jar of honey sent by Maisie at Eleanor's request. Richard's collar was now sticking to the weeping burns on his neck and had to be carefully removed. Even though Joan and Eleanor performed the delicate operation as gently as they could it still caused poor Richard a considerable amount of pain; however, he consoled himself with the fact that he was still alive to feel the pain. The slashed shirt was removed and a clean one sent for while the two ladies cleaned his wounds and applied the honey to prevent any infection, and to aid the healing. A clean dressing was finally applied before he slipped on his fresh shirt, feeling much more comfortable.

It was a very thankful and light-hearted group that assembled in the dining room for supper that evening. Richard's meal had to be mashed into something little more than a pulp, but he managed to swallow it without too much difficulty by taking his time. He hoped it wouldn't be too long before he was tucking into a proper meal like everyone else.

After their post-dinner drink in the parlour, Richard and Joan went to the kitchen to see the staff. Joan, as promised, briefly explained what had happened at Sir Richard's trial and that he had been exonerated, pardoned and released by order of the Queen. Everyone cheered and Giles offered a toast to the master. They all raised their tankards, drank to Richard's release and cheered again. Richard thanked them with a brief nod but his eyes were full as he turned to take Joan's hand before they left for the parlour.

In the morning, Edmund and Eleanor departed for Holyfield in a much happier state of mind. Will went off to the office cheerfully, reassuring Richard that he could cope without him until he had recovered his voice. He promised to bring home any documents that needed Richard's signature. Not long after everyone had left Richard began to get restless. Joan asked him if he would like to take a walk in the garden with her but he shook his head and left the room. She laughed when he returned carrying his riding boots under his arm and holding his whip in his hand.

"Just give me five minutes to change and I'll meet you at the stables," she said.

By the time she joined them, both Diablo and Caesar where saddled and ready to go. Although Richard couldn't speak, he was still enjoying a croaky laugh with Sam and Barnaby as he waited for Joan. Once through the gate they set off at a moderate pace. Joan deliberately held back as she assumed that Richard would need a few days to recover from his ordeal in Exeter, but when they had travelled about a mile down the road Richard suddenly tapped Diablo's flanks with his heels. That was all the encouragement his horse needed to set off at the gallop towards the fields and a breakneck race across the countryside. Richard led them to the clifftops where they dismounted, laughing and out of breath. They stood for a while looking out to sea with an arm around each other.

"Now you are convinced that you really are free, aren't you?"

He knew that his lovely wife would understand. He turned her to face him. "I love you!" he mouthed before kissing her passionately.

Over the coming weeks Richard recovered his voice, albeit with a lower pitch and slightly gravelly. At first he was self-conscious about these changes and tried to avoid speaking. To help him become more confident in his speech, Joan coaxed him into having conversations not only with his family and servants, but also with anyone else he came into contact with on the estate. She knew that her perseverance and patience had paid off when he finally told her that he felt ready to work again.

The day before Richard's planned return to the office, Will arrived home with a letter from his friend John, William Cecil's clerk.

"Remember, Richard, you met John when you first came to Court," Will said. "He sent this with a royal courier who was delivering papers and documents to several places in Devon. John gave the man a few extra coins to take a slight detour to deliver his letter to me in Topsham! It's a narrative of what happened between Her Majesty and Sir Francis Walsingham after she had discovered that you had been sentenced to death for treason. It's all true because John witnessed it with his own eyes—he was actually in the Queen's private apartments with Cecil. While Her Majesty and her secretary discussed the various documents she wanted Cecil to prepare John was writing down notes and instructions. When Walsingham was announced the Queen flew into such a rage John thinks that she forgot that he was there. Now just listen to this."

With that, Will began to read John's account.

*"There you are, Walsingham, you wretch! How dare you put me in the position of having to counter one of the most serious laws in the land. I was compelled by the most urgent of circumstances to countermand a legal decision made in a court of law. My court and my law, you imbecile! Don't stand there staring me down as if you have no idea what I'm referring to, you simpleton!"*

*"Forgive me, Your Majesty,"* Walsingham stammered, *"but I have no idea what you are talking about."*

*"Don't lie to me, you snake! Do you really expect me to believe that you had no knowledge of Sir Richard Lovell's trial and death sentence? You must think me a fool!"*

*Walsingham fell to knees. "Your Grace, please believe me when I say that I know nothing of this happening."*

*"Did you or did you not coerce Richard into allowing traitors to be ferried into my realm on his*

ships, where they were met by a Spanish agent who forwarded them on further into the country to create God knows what mischief?" Here Elizabeth picked up a fancy box from her table and hurled it at him. Her ladies were huddled together in a corner as they knew the extent of their mistress's fiery, violent temper. Cecil and I had moved our stools from the line of fire and were sitting beside a wall close to the ladies. "Well? Answer me!" she commanded.

"Your majesty, I can assure you that all these agents are being closely watched, as are their accomplices and sympathisers. When the time is right they will all be arrested, King Philip's plan of subversion thwarted and your realm a much safer place because of it," Sir Francis insisted.

"That may be so, but what of Richard? Did you think his life was expendable to further your scheme?"

"As I said, your majesty, I didn't know that he had been arrested."

"And if you had, would you have lifted a finger to save him, or would you have turned your back and let him suffer a traitor's death, knowing that all he was guilty of was following your instructions?"

Walsingham hesitated, which infuriated the Queen. "You ingrate! You insufferable toad! That man has already risked his life to save mine! His father risked his life for my sake, too, albeit in a different way!"

Another missile was thrown at Walsingham. He ducked out of its way before the precious object smashed to pieces on the floor. "Because of you *an innocent man almost lost his life in the worst manner possible. I will not have it. Walsingham!"* she screeched.

*"My dread sovereign, everything I do and the methods I use are solely for your protection and the safety of your realm. We live in very dangerous times and risks must be taken to keep you safe."*

*"I understand that many of your methods are underhanded, but hear me, Walsingham—Sir Richard Lovell is now under my protection and you will not involve him in any of your scheming again! If I hear anything to the contrary, I promise you will pay a very heavy penalty! Do I make myself clear?"*

*"Perfectly clear, Your Majesty,"* replied Walsingham.

*"Good! Now get out of my sight! Go!"* she shouted and threw another object at him as he backed away towards the door.

Smiling, Will said, "John also adds that Joan's letter arrived when Walsingham was away and Phellips took it upon himself to read it. He had never liked the way Sir Francis treated Richard and took the letter to Cecil. On numerous occasions the Queen had mentioned to Cecil how fond she was of Richard and his father, as well as Joan. Cecil knew she would never allow Richard to die because of Walsingham, so he took the letter to her. She then acted on the information immediately and prayed that if the worst had happened and Richard had been found guilty that her messenger would reach Exeter in time to prevent a great injustice.

"So there you have it!" Will concluded triumphantly. "Now we know why it was the Queen who stepped in to save you, Richard, and not Walsingham."

"This means that we are free of Walsingham forever, Richard!" Joan exclaimed. "You are now under the Queen's protection. That loathsome man will never be able to blackmail you again!"

"That's wonderful news," Richard agreed. "Nicholas also seems to have disappeared. He hasn't been seen since I was arrested, and there have been no more agents arriving through Topsham! Dare we believe that our lives are at last our own again?"

At last Richard returned to his work in the shipping office. As Will brought him up to date, Richard found himself impressed by Will's diligence. Clearly his decision to give Will the chance to redeem himself had been the right one. When they had dealt with the most pressing tasks Richard decided that he would go and find the men who had testified against him, to reassure them that he harboured no ill feeling—after all, they were only telling the truth as they saw it. Will invited himself along, wanting to check on a ship that was due to leave for the Netherlands carrying bundles of fleeces.

As they drew level with the ship Will noticed two huge bales hanging on the end of the crane's chain. Without warning, the crane swung round towards him and Richard with such force that he only had a second to push Richard out of the way before he himself was hit by the full impact of the load. Richard landed flat on his face but was otherwise uninjured—while his clerk lay unconscious in the ship's hold. As Richard scrambled into the hold he shouted for someone to find a physician.

Will bled profusely from a deep gash in his head and was lying with one arm under him and one of his legs twisted at an unnatural angle. There was no sign of life as Richard tried to stem the bleeding.

After what seemed an age the physician arrived, complaining that he had been almost press-ganged into accompanying the sailors. However, when the man saw the state Will was in, he snapped into action. A makeshift stretcher was constructed from things the sailors found in the hold, and with Richard's help the physician managed to staunch the bleeding long enough to inspect the gash. It was long and deep and had grazed the skull but hadn't penetrated the bone. Both the arm and leg were broken but after a swift examination it was decided that the breaks were clean and that the bones should knit together properly if Will did as he was told. It was when the sailors lifted Will onto the stretcher that the physician noticed the swelling on the side of his head. Will had received a hefty blow and although the skin hadn't been broken the physician was worried that there could be internal bruising—or worse still, internal bleeding.

The doctor accompanied Will and Richard to the manor, Will carefully laid out in the back of a wagon with the physician in attendance, Richard riding Diablo and leading Will's horse. Once they had settled Will in his bed, the doctor stitched the gash and set the broken bones before he splinted them. Will still hadn't regained consciousness and the physician was becoming concerned about the lump on the side of his head. Before he departed, he left precise instructions for Will's care and promised to return the following day. Richard escorted the doctor to the stables and arranged for Sam to take him back to Topsham in the coach. He then told Barnaby to saddle Diablo again before he returned to the house.

"I'm going to Exeter to see Will's father," Richard told Joan. "He must be told what's happened to his son. I'll also send Barnaby to fetch my mother. She will stay with you and help to nurse Will until I return."

"But, Richard, it will be almost dark by the time you reach Exeter," Joan protested.

"I know, my love. I will stay at an inn overnight and return home as early as possible tomorrow."

He gathered a few things, gave Joan a parting kiss and headed out. In Exeter he made his way to the glovemaker's residence. William Perceval senior lived in a large house in one of the better areas of the town, not far from where he plied his successful trade of making the best quality gloves for royalty, the nobility and gentry.

Richard was greeted at the door by the steward, who left him in the entrance hall. When the steward returned, he ushered Richard into a parlour far more luxurious than his own. Will's father stood and welcomed him with a firm handshake. "Richard, how nice to see you again, and all grown up!" he exclaimed. "The last time we met you were still attending the grammar school here in Exeter."

"Indeed, sir, it was."

"I can see by your expression that this is not a social call," Perceval said. "As my son now works for and resides with you, I can only surmise that this visit has something to do with him. If you have come to intercede for him, I made my feelings on the matter clear the last time we met, and they have not changed. I am ashamed to call him my son. If that was the purpose of your visit then I am afraid you've wasted your time."

"I am here because your son is at this moment fighting for his life after saving mine," Richard told him.

Will's father staggered back into his chair. "Is he so very badly hurt? What happened to him?"

Richard told Perceval how Will had taken the blow from the crane to save him. William sat silently for a few moments, before he said, "When will you be returning to the manor? I would like to accompany you if that is permissible?"

At Richard's explanation that he intended to take a room at an inn and leave at first light, William insisted he stay at the family home. They would leave together the following day.

Richard and William spoke until late into the night. Richard shared with him how Walsingham had blackmailed him into taking part in dangerous schemes, with the threat that Edmund's business would suffer otherwise. Will had faced the same choice with Nicholas; he was forced to betray Richard to save his father from harm. Understandably, Will's love for his father had overridden all else—even his friendship with Richard, who he thought of almost as a brother. At last, it seemed, William grasped the situation his son had found himself in.

They set out early in the morning. When they reached the manor, they were told Will's condition hadn't changed. Eleanor and Joan had taken it in turns to watch over the patient through the night, and the physician had already been and left. The doctor was concerned that Will still hadn't regained consciousness but was satisfied that his other injuries would heal. Eleanor had brought a jar of her arnica ointment with her from Holyfield and explained to the physician how it had once helped to reduce the huge swelling on the back of Richard's head after his fall from his horse. The man didn't think it would do any harm and so Eleanor had covered the lump with a copious amount of the salve and enclosed it in a clean dressing.

Eleanor was with Will when his father was shown into the room, still wearing his cloak and riding boots. William was shocked to see his son so pale, his head bandaged and his arm in a sling; he rushed to the bedside and sat down next to him, taking his son's hand in his. Eleanor made to leave, to give them privacy, but Perceval stopped her with the question, "Is he going to die, Eleanor? Am I going to lose him before I get the chance to admit what a fool I have been? When he told me what he had done all I could think of was that he had not only betrayed Walsingham's trust but also Richard's in such a way that he could have completely ruined all of you. It was just too much to take in. Although he tried to explain why, I couldn't make sense of it. I was so angry all I could think of was that he was a traitor—my son, a traitor. I said some very hateful things to him. Things a father should never say to a son. Am I now too late to put that right?"

"I hope not, William, but we will have to wait and see," Eleanor gently answered.

"Yes, yes indeed," William said, and turned back toward his son. He was still in the same position hours later when Joan arrived to take her turn watching over the patient.

This was the pattern for the next twenty-four hours, with no change in Will's condition. Finally, while William was watching over his son, he felt Will give his hand a weak squeeze. A few seconds later Will's eyes opened and blinked at the light. "Father?" he asked. "Is that really you?"

"Yes, son, it's really me," said William, laughing and crying at the same time. "Oh, my dear son, you have come back to me! I was terrified that I'd lost you!" He shouted loudly for Eleanor. She rushed into the room closely followed by Richard and Joan all fearing the worst. They were delighted to see Will awake. It was only when he tried to sit up that he realised his arm and leg were in splints.

He dizzily fell back onto his pillow.

"That's quite enough of that," Eleanor admonished him as she fussed about his bed, plumping up his pillows and straightening the covers. "If you want to mend properly you are going to have to do as you're told for a while yet, young man."

Will looked helplessly at Richard.

"It's no use looking at me," laughed Richard, "I would never dare to disobey her when she's in this mood!"

Eleanor left to find Will some food. Joan and Richard similarly excused themselves, leaving father and son alone to reconcile.

When Richard returned later in the day, he found Will alone and lying with his eyes closed. Not wanting to disturb him he turned towards the door and made to leave. "I'm not sleeping, just resting," murmured Will. "Please stay."

Richard sat in the chair beside the bed. "I've seen you looking better, my friend," he remarked, "but at least you are in a much healthier condition than when you were in the bottom of the ship's hold. Honestly, Will, I thought you were dead. I owe you my life and I can't put a price on that. Thank you."

Smiling, Will answered, "Don't pretend you wouldn't have done the same for me, Richard. I know you too well for you to deny it!"

Richard squeezed Will's shoulder before he said, "I have just returned from Topsham and I am afraid I have disturbing news. What happened was not an accident. Apparently the two men who should have been manning the crane had been bribed to disappear. Three men were working the crane when you were hit. That was why the force of the blow was so strong—but it was meant for me, not you. Needless to say, those men have long gone but the two who were bribed stupidly came back to resume their work with the crane. You'll be pleased to know that they no longer work for me nor will they ever work on the dock again."

"Dear God, Richard!" Will exclaimed. "Who wants you dead? You were cleared of the treason charge! You are no longer involved with Walsingham and Nicholas has gone."

"I have no idea. I've been asking myself the same question over and over again. It doesn't make any sense. However, it's not for you to worry about. You need to concentrate on getting well again as soon as possible. Take heed of my mother's instructions or you'll be sorry. She has a tongue as sharp as any sword if you don't comply," chuckled Richard. "I'll leave you to rest. That is the best medicine you can have."

Richard left Will, and then sent Agnes in search of Joan with a message to meet him in the garden.

Joan found her husband, deep in thought, sitting on a garden seat. "What's wrong my love? You look distressed," she said.

With a sigh, Richard answered, "I believe someone wants me dead."

"What! That can't be right!" Joan protested. "Who would want that? We're out of Walsingham's schemes now. Why would anyone want to kill you?"

When Richard told Joan about the men operating the crane, Joan groaned. "I thought all that was behind us now," she protested. "Do we need to start looking over our shoulders and jumping at shadows again? I'm not sure I can go through that anymore. I thought that part of our lives was over."

Richard put his arm around her shoulder and pulled her close. "I'm sorry, my darling. The damnable thing is I have no idea who I'm looking for. Nor do I know if it's just me they want dead, or if it involves you and young Edmund too. Until we know, I think we should continue keeping our fighting skills at the highest level and remain vigilant."

"We will be completely on our own this time,"

Joan stated. "If Walsingham isn't involved, his men won't be watching over us."

"I know, and the thought terrifies me," Richard admitted. "However, I'd rather we didn't say anything to the parents yet. It would only worry them, and until we can uncover the truth, they couldn't do anything to help."

"Yes, but what about us? We can't sit doing nothing until there's another attempt on your life," Joan argued. "Next time they might be successful."

"I'm afraid we have no choice, my love. Since we have no idea who they are we must wait until they make their move and hope that we can thwart it. Until then we must put our faith in God that He will protect us and keep us safe."

When they re-joined the others in the parlour, they presented two cheerful faces. No-one had any idea of their sombre conversation in the garden— or that Richard's life was once again in danger.

Will improved a little every day. The lump receded, the stitched gash healed and his bones knitted together again but it was a long process.

The Yule had come and gone before Will was fit to return to the office. While his clerk recovered Richard went into his office every day to keep his business running smoothly. Whenever a stranger appeared he was instantly on his guard, and when he was out and about in the town, he regarded everyone with suspicion. The constant stress was becoming a heavy burden.

One morning he was considering shutting the office for an hour so that he could speak with Lorenzo about continuing his and Joan's lessons, when the man himself appeared.

"Lorenzo, well met my friend!" Richard exclaimed. "I was about to come to the fencing school to have a few words with you. What can I do for you?"

"Nothing at present," he replied, "but later I would be grateful for your moral support. I am certain Francesca will be glad of Joan's, as well, when her time comes."

"Are you saying what I think you are?" asked Richard with a wide grin.

"Yes indeed!" Lorenzo proudly answered. "Francesca is with child."

Richard stood and shook his friend's hand vigorously. "Congratulations! I am so pleased for you both. Joan will be delighted when she hears your wonderful news."

"Thank you! But you said you were about to come to see me. Is there anything amiss?"

Richard explained to Lorenzo what had happened on the dock, and how Will had pushed him out of the way, at a great cost to himself.

"Are you sure that it wasn't just a terrible accident, Richard?" asked Lorenzo. "Is it possible that the crane operators had just lost control of the load?"

"It was no accident. I discovered later that the

three men responsible were not my employees. My own men had been bribed to leave their post. It was attempted murder but I don't know on whose instructions or why," Richard said. "I was coming to discuss with you the possibility of Joan and me resuming our lessons. I had hoped those days were behind us, but in light of this attempt I believe we must be ready to defend ourselves."

"You are right, of course, but there is nothing more I can teach Joan. I will spar with her to sharpen her reactions and to keep her on her toes. You, on the other hand, still have skills to learn and more to practice. I will be honest with you, my friend—you will never be as proficient as your wife, but when we are finished you will be more than ready to defend yourself against all but the very best swordsmen."

Lorenzo had not long left the office when a courier arrived from London. Richard's heart sank. What would he do if his presence was required in London? He couldn't leave Topsham until Will was fit enough to take up his duties again, and he couldn't really ask his father to step in, as Edmund was busy setting up the new farms. With much trepidation he broke the seal on the letter. It was from Hubert .Why was he sending a message now? The ships wouldn't be returning for weeks yet. His heart skipped a beat.

As he read, however, a smile crept over his face.

Hubert apologised for sending the message now instead of after the ships had returned, but he wanted to share his exciting news with Richard. He had fallen in love with the girl whose family lived downstairs—the same girl who had nursed him back to health after his attack. They planned to marry in the late summer of the following year. Hubert fervently hoped that Sir Richard and Lady Joan would be able to attend the wedding ceremony. He intended to invite Lord and Lady Lovell as well, although he appreciated it was a considerable journey for them to make.

Richard was still smiling as he folded the missive and placed it in his pocket. What wonderful news he would have for Joan when he returned home today—a welcome change from worrying about where the next attempt on his life would come from.

# CHAPTER 11

Joan was delighted to hear Lorenzo's news, but silently prayed that Francesca would not experience the same trauma she had with baby Edmund. She was also thrilled that Hubert planned to get married and overjoyed that she and Richard had been invited to attend. Most exciting of all the wedding would be in London. Although she would never admit it to Richard, she did miss the city and its busyness. The thought of seeing old friends again filled her with joy.

Will recovered well from his horrendous injuries, thanks to Eleanor and Joan's strict nursing. Before he returned to his work in Topsham, he spent a few days with his father in Exeter. Both men were grateful to be reconciled again, and to have recovered their close relationship.

Richard and Joan recommenced their lessons with Lorenzo as a precaution against their high level of skills falling. Meanwhile, Edmund and Eleanor were kept busy with their new farming venture. Eleanor had tired of staying behind at

Holyfield while her husband was out and about overseeing the work. In years past, she'd had Richard to care for. Now Eleanor had no ties and was determined to join her husband whenever she could, to support and offer him advice—whether it was called for or not.

The building of the new farmhouses had been progressing at pace thanks to the unexpectedly calm, dry weather. Edmund was hoping it might be the sign of an early spring. After the Yuletide he'd ordered the necessary farm equipment from the local blacksmith, he'd sourced the required seed in Exeter and he'd acquired a few cows, pigs and chickens to be raised on the farms. Fortunately, he had retained enough sheep to give each farm their own small flock.

Richard and Edmund chose the most able families to run the farms on their behalf and gifted each village their own piece of land for the growing of their own food. The villagers were delighted that there would now be so much work to do their children would no longer have to leave home in search of employment.

By mid-spring, after an incredible amount of hard work, the farmhouses were occupied and the fields planted. Pens were ready to receive the livestock and the children were kept busy scaring away the birds which would eat the seed or the young shoots. The villagers spent many backbreaking hours weeding the fields to give the crops every chance to produce a high yield at harvest time.

Richard had been happy to let his father take charge of the farms as his main interest had always been in the shipping side of the business, but he hadn't expected the experience to put such a spring in Edmund's step. In fact, both his mother and father seemed invigorated by the challenge, and he was delighted to see it.

When Will returned to work, Richard was able to take extra time off to spend with his family. Sadly, their blissful Utopia was soon once again turned on its head.

One morning just after Richard finished dressing, Giles informed him that Sam urgently needed to speak with him. Sam had refused to come into the house; he was standing outside the kitchen door when Richard arrived. As he stepped out of the kitchen Sam backed away. "Please, Sir Richard," he said, "don't come any closer."

Alarmed "What's wrong?" Richard asked, retreating back into the kitchen. "Has something happened to your mother?"

"No, sir, my ma is well, or at least I hope she is," Sam answered. "There are cases of measles in the village. Many of the children are already sick and some adults, too. Although my ma and me are almost sure that we haven't been in close contact with any of them I don't want to take any chances. I'll eat and sleep in the stable until I'm sure I'm not infected. I would hate anything to happen to your son because of me."

"Thank you, Sam," Richard said. "I think that's exactly what you should do. But what about Barnaby?"

"It shouldn't affect him, sir. He had the measles many years ago when he worked at Holyfield Hall."

"Very well. We will follow that plan until we know one way or the other," Richard said. "Thank you for bringing the information to me."

When Richard shared Sam's news with Joan, the colour drained from her face. "What about Edmund?" she said. "What will we do if he gets sick? Oh, dear God, what if he dies? Richard, I'm frightened."

"Thanks to Sam we now have time to put precautions in place to prevent the disease from entering the manor," Richard reassured her. "Tell Agnes I wish to speak to all the servants in the kitchen as soon as possible. Let me know when they are assembled."

In the nursery Richard told Edmund's nurse Mary that neither she nor Edmund was to leave the house for any reason without his express permission. Joan joined them after sending Agnes on her way. "You must watch Edmund very carefully for any signs that he is unwell," Joan told the nurse. "Inform me immediately if there is."

Joan and Richard then went to the kitchen, where the servants were gathered. Richard told them that no-one was to enter or leave the manor without his permission. Anything delivered to the manor was to be left outside the gate and collected. The food already stored at the manor would feed everyone for a few weeks if the portions were rationed.

Richard and Joan decided that Will should stay at The Bush for the next couple of weeks, in case the epidemic arrived in Topsham and he inadvertently brought it back to the manor with him. Will agreed to the plan and packed what he would need into his saddlebags before he left for the office.

When Richard was sure he had done all he could to protect his household, he prepared to wait for matters take their own course.

After a few days had passed and no-one was feeling ill or showing any symptoms, Richard decided that he and Joan could safely take a ride in the country. Joan was reluctant to go at first, but Richard convinced her that they both needed some fresh air and that Edmund would be quite safe at home.

They arrived back at the stable refreshed and revitalised. After a short conversation with Barnaby and Sam, Richard and Joan returned to the house where Giles and Henry met them. Joan sensed immediately that something was wrong and although she had already guessed what it was, she was still shocked to hear that Edmund was showing symptoms. She ran to the nursery, Richard close behind. They heard Edmund's pitiful cries long before they reached the door; when they entered they saw the nurse cradling the boy, rocking him backwards and forwards in an attempt to calm him. When Joan took her son from Mary, she could feel the heat radiating from him. His face was flushed, his eyes were red, and he was feverish.

Joan looked helplessly at Richard, as the baby kept sobbing as if his little heart would break.

"I'll go for my mother," he said. "She'll know what to do."

"Wait!" Joan cried. "What if Eleanor hasn't had the measles and she catches it from Edmund? We cannot allow her to be exposed too! We might lose them both!"

"I believe she and my father must have been infected at some point in their lives, as neither became ill when I had measles as a child," Richard assured her. "I presume you had them at the same time as Barnaby."

Joan paled. "No, I did not. Geoffrey and I were kept closeted away from the servants when it came to Holyfield Hall. Many of the servants came down with it, and three of the younger ones died. It was horrible. Father also cruelly dismissed two of the servants when it was over, as one had been left deaf and the other blind."

"Good God, Joan, you could become ill too! I'm going to Holyfield now. Look after Edmund and I will return as quickly as I can."

With that Richard left for his parents' home. The hours began to feel like years for Joan as she nursed her little son. He had now started to cough in between his sobbing, and he rubbed his eyes whenever he managed to get his hand free. His fever also appeared to be increasing.

It was a relief when Eleanor rushed into the room with her little bag of potions and herbs closely followed by Richard. She felt the little one's forehead and checked his eyes; when she loosened the blanket to check him for spots he began to cough. She was tut-tutting all the time as she was examining her grandson's body. "I presume you that you checked his mouth," Eleanor said to Mary, as she gently opened the infant's mouth and peered inside.

"Yes, my lady, but there weren't any spots there. I did look carefully."

"Not for spots—for teeth! The poor child is cutting two back molars at the same time. They aren't quite through the gum yet and will be causing Edmund considerable pain, hence all the tears. The constant crying will have eventually made him cough and irritated his eyes. The fever too is part of the teething process."

Joan turned on Mary. "You should have realised that you stupid girl!" Before she could say anymore the nurse burst into tears and hurriedly left the room.

Eleanor turned to Joan. "He doesn't have measles, Joan. He is just teething, although that can sometimes be almost as distressing. Now let's give him something to bring down his fever and calm those sore gums."

When his grandmama's treatment had calmed Edmund enough for Joan to settle him down to sleep Richard gently took her to one side. "Don't you think you were a little harsh with Mary, my love? You had instructed her to inform you immediately if Edmund began to show symptoms of the measles and that is precisely what she did. You held the boy in your arms until mother arrived. Did you once check to see if he was teething?"

"No of course not! I was terrified that he had the measles and might die!"

"Exactly, and Mary loves him almost as much as we do. She too would have been frightened of losing him."

"Oh Richard, I was so worried about Edmund I never gave a thought to Mary's feelings. Poor girl. I will go and find her and apologise," she promised remorsefully.

Fortunately, the ministrations worked, and life at the manor soon calmed down again. It was almost two weeks later that they received word from the village that the measles epidemic was deemed over. The messenger also brought news of Sam's mother. She was alive and well, having been a great asset to the villagers by nursing the sick and comforting the bereaved.

Richard lost no time in riding to Topsham to tell Will that it was safe for him to return home. He was surprised to discover that Captain Ashe had already arrived from London, carrying the money transfer document and the usual letters from Thomas and Margaret. Indeed, Tom was still at The Bush, having chosen to remain until he could speak to his employer. Richard went to The Bush immediately and was lucky enough to catch his captain on his way out.

Tom quickly brought Richard up to date. The ships were back in port with full cargos. It had not all been smooth sailing, however: The Bonaventure had been attacked by pirates early on in their journey home. The Edmund and The Eleanor Joan were several miles behind at the time, but when the pirates saw the other ships approaching, they broke off the attack and fled.

The Bonaventure crew had put up a good defence, especially One-Eyed-Jack; his performance had inspired the crew to fight back. Sadly, one sailor had lost his life and another was seriously injured. Still, Tom was convinced that if the other two ships hadn't been nearby, his ship would have been overwhelmed.

Richard was both shocked and troubled.

"I know it isn't standard practice to have soldiers on a cargo ship," Tom told him, "but I believe that a couple of good bowmen on board would have made all the difference. There are many ex-soldiers wandering the land looking for employment and I wondered if it would be feasible to employ two on each ship. We could bring along a small armoury of extra weapons for the crew as well, while the bowmen could also serve as extra crew members."

"It's certainly something worth thinking about," Richard mused, "but you would need to ensure they could shoot straight and that they would be prepared to serve under the same conditions as the rest of the crew."

"I could do that," Tom assured him. "With your permission, I would also like to issue an order your behalf to the effect that in future all the vessels must remain in sight of each other at all times."

"Good idea, Tom. Permission granted. I will leave all the new arrangements to you. By the way, are you not supposed to be on shore leave?" Richard asked him.

"Aye, sir. I've been catching up with old friends and going over past times with them over a jug or two, if you know what I mean," Tom replied with a broad grin. "Now I have spoken to you, I'll be leaving for London tomorrow to find our bowmen, get the ships loaded and be on our way."

"Before you go, tell me—how did Matthew get on with The Edmund?"

"He's a good man sir. He handled his ship and his crew admirably, so much so that the whole crew signed on for the next voyage. I'm certain he'll do very well for you."

"Good! I'm pleased to hear it. I'll not detain you any longer, then," Richard said. "Once again, I am in your debt. Thank you."

Richard returned to his office and carefully

checked the figures relating to the latest cargo sales. He was thrilled to discover that after expenses he and his father had once again made a hefty profit, but paused to consider just how different it would have been had they lost The Bonaventure. It was not unknown for pirates not only to take the cargo but commandeer the ship as well. He hoped that Tom's extra precautions would prevent such a disastrous outcome in the future.

In the morning Richard and Will went into Topsham together. After they dropped off their horses off at stables, they saw a familiar figure striding towards them.

"Well, Richard," Nicholas said, his sickening smile in place, "I see that you are no longer hiding yourself away at the manor."

"I was hardly hiding," Richard retorted. "I was protecting my family and household from the measles epidemic."

"If you say so…although I've heard that you now crouch behind our illustrious majesty's petticoats."

Richard reached for the hilt of his sword. "I hide from no-one, least of all the likes of you!"

"Oh, don't be such a fool, man!" Nicholas laughed. "You know that you are no match for me. However, if you would care to try I'm sure that I could make a better job of despatching you than those idiots on the crane." Richard was shocked.

"How did you know I would be there on that

day? I hadn't been at the office for weeks!"

"Because I'd had the manor watched every day awaiting your return to Topsham. The men had been briefed to man the crane as soon as you appeared and to use it to kill you at the first opportunity. You are a marked man Richard but me running you through would be too easy. Your end will come out of the blue when you are least expecting it—and have no fear Richard, next time we will not fail. You will be quite alone when the deed is done, with no misguided employee there to save your miserable skin." He gave Will a murderous look.

Richard yearned to thrust his sword through the braggard's heart but knew he would be dead long before his weapon reached its target. "It was on your orders that an attempt was made on my life, you bastard!" he spit out. "Why? I'm no threat to you. I'm no longer involved with your mission."

"Because, my friend, from the first time I set eyes on your lovely wife I was determined to take her for myself," Nicholas answered with a wink. "But of course, I can't do that while you still dwell in this world, so go you must."

Furious, Richard shot back, "You must be mad to think Joan would let you anywhere near her. She would die rather than surrender herself to you, you murdering scum!"

"If she wants to see her son live and thrive, she will do anything I command," Nicholas sneered vindictively and continued on his way, laughing as he went.

Horrified, Will said to Richard, "You must tell the authorities about his threats to your life and have him arrested!"

"We can prove nothing. Besides," Richard added bitterly, "he's under Walsingham's protection until the trap is slammed shut. Hopefully when that happens it will bring about the end of the assassin. There is nothing we can do for the moment except to be ever more vigilant."

Richard felt a stab of despair, wondering just what else he could do to keep himself safe, but at least now he knew it was only his life in danger. At the same time, he was well aware of what would happen to Joan if Nicholas succeeded with his plan. Lord de Luc was an old man when she was almost forced to marry him, but Nicholas was young, with many years ahead of him. Richard couldn't bear the thought and hoped that Joan would run away with Edmund before Nicholas reached her. Yet if the Spanish invaded, provoking insurrections everywhere, where could she flee to that would be safe?

Joan was appalled when Richard told her about his encounter with Nicholas. She was more than a little frightened, too. It seemed as if she and Richard had stumbled from one crisis to another ever since the day they had met.

She was only slightly relieved when Nicholas wasn't seen in Topsham in the weeks following his altercation with Richard although she was well aware that Nicholas didn't need to be present in order to arrange for her husband's assassination and it terrified her.

As the year moved forward without further attempts on Richard's life, he and Joan began to relax, just a little. So far the weather had been exceptionally kind, and it was looking as if the farms would produce bumper crops in their first year. Everyone prayed that the perfect conditions would continue at least until after the harvest.

One morning in late summer Lorenzo rushed into Richard's office and announced that Francesca was in labour. He'd sent for the midwife and urged his friend to fetch Joan as quickly as possible; Francesca was already starting to panic about the birth, and Joan would comfort her.

Diablo seemed to sense the urgency and made short work of the journey. Joan was alarmed when Richard shared the news; Francesca wasn't due for several weeks yet. She was also concerned that the baby would be too big for her friend to deliver. Considering the stature of her friend, the baby already appeared to be quite large.

As she changed her clothes to ride to Topsham, Joan put all those thoughts to the back of her mind. She collected her little bag of herbs and oils and dashed to the stable where Barnaby already had Caesar saddled and waiting.

When they reached Lorenzo's house, Joan ran up the stairs to the bedchamber. The midwife was already attending to Francesca, but the frightened young woman was relieved to see her friend. As the pain became stronger and more frequent, Joan massaged scented oil into Francesca's aching back, and encouraged her to listen to the midwife's instructions. Her calm voice disguised her own concern. If the worst were to happen, would she have the strength to comfort her dear friend as she passed from this world to the next? No, Joan chided herself, she mustn't think like that. Francesca would live—she had to.

Time went on and the pain became more intense. Francesca gripped Joan's hand so tightly she thought that her finger's would break under the pressure. Every so often the midwife would feel around Francesca's big bump, frowning. Eventually there must have been some change because the midwife let out a sigh of relief. When she checked for signs that the birth was in progress, she announced in a relieved voice "Baby's on the way! When you feel the urge, Francesca, you must bear down and push."

Unfortunately, the baby was in no hurry to be born. Francesca had another two hours of torment to suffer before her baby finally completed its journey into the world.

"You have a fine son, my dear," clucked the midwife, as she cut the cord and laid the babe across Francesca's chest. Joan and Francesca were both in tears as they greeted the new-born before the midwife took him away to clean him and wrap him in swaddling.

Confused, Francesca said, "I feel as though I want to push again."

"You still need to expel the placenta, child," explained the older woman. However, when she checked below the sheet again, she exclaimed, "Oh my! I think you have been keeping a secret, my dear. There's another little one on the way!"

Joan was absolutely amazed, and poor Francesca utterly shocked. After only a few contractions the second babe made her appearance while showing off her strong vocal chords, much to Joan's amusement. Although smaller than average both babies were perfect and healthy.

Once the bedding had been changed and Francesca washed and changed into a fresh nightgown her babies were placed into her arms. After kissing her little miracles she asked Joan and the midwife to take the babies to meet their father.

The midwife entered the parlour first, carrying the boy.

"Say hello to your son," she said, as she put the child into his father's arms.

Lorenzo was spellbound. "He is wonderful!"

"He certainly is," agreed Richard, peering over his friend's shoulder. "What are you going to name him?"

"Why, Lorenzo of course," Lorenzo replied, his eyes misting over.

Just then Joan entered the parlour. "And what

will you be naming your beautiful daughter?" she asked as she approached him with another precious little bundle.

"Two?" he said, looking from one to the other. He passed his son to Richard and carefully took his daughter from Joan "Isn't she incredible?" he marvelled, and gently kissed her forehead. "She's a miniature Francesca!"

"So it's to be Lorenzo and Francesca then!" Richard said with a grin.

"No, my friend," Lorenzo answered. "It will be Lorenzo and Giovanna."

"Giovanna! What a pretty name," Joan remarked.

"Yes, it is! It is the Italian name for Joan," Lorenzo told her.

"Oh, Lorenzo," Joan gasped. "I am honoured, but are you sure?"

"Of course. If it wasn't for you and Richard, we would never have found each other again. We both decided that if the baby was a girl she would be named Giovanna after our dearest friend and my finest student." Lorenzo leaned forward and gave Joan a kiss on her cheek. "How is Francesca? Can I see her now?"

"Your wife is very well and by now will be patiently waiting to see her husband and to have her babies back," the midwife answered. Joan took baby Lorenzo from Richard and everyone followed the midwife back up the stairs to the bedchamber where Francesca was eagerly awaiting their arrival.

Richard gave Francesca a peck on her cheek and offered his congratulations. Joan handed Lorenzo back to his mother and left with Richard, leaving the new parents with their little family.

In the weeks the followed, the late summer and autumn proved busy times for the family. Their farms had been blessed with a bumper harvest, and it took a great deal of work to gather everything in before the weather turned. The villagers' own fields had done just as well. There would be no empty bellies on either estate during the coming winter.

Edmund had commissioned the building of a watermill that was now situated beside the river that ran through his estate. Holyfield Hall already boasted a large bakehouse where the flour could then be made into bread, and Richard was planning on having a purpose-built bake house constructed at the manor, as well as a dairy.

The cost of the watermill had almost emptied the coffers, so it was a huge relief to hear that the three ships had docked safely with their holds overflowing with lucrative cargoes. Letters arrived as usual from Margaret to Joan, and for Richard from Captain Ashe. Captain Ashe wrote:

> Sir Richard, you will be pleased to hear that there were no incidents on this voyage. Even the winds were kind, following us all the way home. The bowmen worked well with the crews who accepted

them happily enough. They did their part on land as well. I have no regrets about signing them on.

The new wharves are progressing well but the winter weather will prevent us from doing very much over the coming months. However, they should be completed by late spring or early summer. The abundance of good wood makes the job easier, especially as it is growing close by and does not require much transport.

I feel I must mention that Thomas's health is beginning to fail. There is not yet cause for alarm, but he tires quickly now and is content to allow George and Margaret to run the store between them. Margaret is also showing her age although she refuses to admit it.

George is now courting a young lass and hopes to marry her. She is a likeable, hardworking girl who is popular with the colonists. It might be worth thinking about allowing them to take over for Thomas and Margaret sooner rather than later, but of course that must be your decision.

You will be amused to hear that One-Eyed-Jack has become smitten with a buxom widow with a family already grown. She has made it very clear that he is wasting his time unless he plans to marry her. He doesn't seem to know what to do. I don't think he has ever fallen for a woman in his life before. Maybe his ardour will have cooled by the time we reach America again.

My regards to you and Lady Joan.

Tom

Richard decided that if Margaret hadn't mentioned anything to Joan about her father's health, he would keep silent for the time being. Tom had said that there was no need to worry, but he was correct Thomas and Margaret would soon need to retire.

Joan and young Edmund had become frequent visitors at Francesca and Lorenzo's home since the birth of the twins. Edmund was fascinated by the two babies. He would stand beside their cribs and watch them sleep, and occasionally stroke their cheeks or give them a little kiss. The first time he heard one of them cry he was so alarmed that he ran to his mother and hid his face in her skirt. When Francesca and his mama sat cradling the babies on their knees, he would shake a little bell rattle; when the babies smiled he would dissolve into fits of chuckles.

One day while sitting on his papa's knee Edmund demanded, "I want a sister, Papa!"

Richard, who was stunned by his son's request, looked imploringly at Joan, sitting opposite him. She was so shocked at her son's sudden statement that she was completely lost for words and just stared back at him open-mouthed.

"I want one now!" Edmund proclaimed. He slid off Richard's knee and stamped his feet.

"Well, I'm afraid you can't have one now!" Richard told him. "It takes time to bring a little sister into the world."

"But I want it NOW!" Edmund screamed.

"Now you listen to me, young man," said Richard, taking hold of his son's shoulders, "You can't always get want you want whenever you want it."

"But I want one now, Papa," Edmund pleaded. He then wrapped his chubby little arms around Richard's neck and began to cry. His Papa gave him a hug.

"You can't have a baby sister now," Richard said looking over Edmund's head towards Joan, "but perhaps later when you are a bit bigger." Joan's eyebrows almost disappeared into her hairline. She stood up and took Edmund's hand. "I think it's time for you to return to the nursery, little man," she said.

"I don't want to!" he protested.

"Mary will be waiting for you with something nice to eat."

"She will?" he asked. When Joan nodded, Edmund quickly said goodbye to his papa and then almost pulled his mama out of the room.

Richard sighed. He then reached for his book and began to read again.

# CHAPTER 12

It was a very happy Yuletide. Richard had been unable to find a suitable pony and there was no baby sister for Edmund but the boy loved his hobbyhorse from his papa. He 'galloped' around the parlour sporting the shirt and breeches his mama and grandmama had made for him. When he was also given his first pair of little leather boots by his grandpapa, Edmund proudly announced that now he was just like his papa. He even went as far as to name his hobbyhorse Diablo, much to everyone's amusement.

However, the gift little Edmund loved best was the wooden cart that Barnaby and Sam had made for him. He spent a long time filling it with the smaller logs that sat beside the fire and carting them around the room before putting them all back again. He repeated the process over and over until Mary collected him and took him to the nursery for his snack and a nap.

After the holidays whenever his nurse took Edmund outdoors for fresh air and exercise the cart went with him. He would wander into the stable dragging it behind him and heave Barnaby's pouch of leather-working tools into it. He would then trundle to the other end of the building where the pouch would be unceremoniously tipped out. If Edmund saw Sam working in the yard he would load that man's tools into the cart too and take them for a tour around the courtyard. He often insisted he 'help' Sam complete whatever task the coachman was busy with.

Edmund's last port of call was usually the kitchen. If he was lucky either Ellen or Maisie would put some sweetmeats or little cakes into his cart. He would then carefully pull his cart into the garden where he would share his spoils with Mary before they returned to the nursery.

Joan often saw her son with the servants while she was carrying out her household duties and she wasn't certain she approved of the amount of time he spent with them. There had been no fraternisation with the servants at Holyfield Hall when she was growing up. Even when young, she and Geoffrey had been treated with deference by the servants, none of whom spoke unless they were spoken to.

At the same time, Joan was aware that her father took a very different view of the serving class than she did but Richard's attitude was even more divergent. Unsure of what to think, she finally broached the subject with Richard. "Do you not think that Edmund is spending far too much time with the servants?" she asked one evening, when they were sitting alone in the parlour. "They seem to be very familiar with him, and he treats them like playmates."

"I have no objection at all to him spending so much time with them, Joan," Richard said easily. "I want him to know our servants and to grow up with a healthy respect for them. Without their service our lives would be very different. He must understand that although they serve, they are not slaves or objects to be used—they are people with emotions and feelings just like us. I am confident that his time spent with them now is time well spent and that he will form many happy memories and learn many lessons for the future." Smiling, Richard added, "It did me no harm. My father's servants loved me as much as our servants love our son."

"I think I understand why you feel that way," Joan said thoughtfully. "The manor is a much happier household than Holyfield Hall ever was. Everyone here does their duties cheerfully and without fear. Yes, you are right. This is exactly the kind of environment I would like our son to grow up in." She gave Richard an apologetic look. "I still find it hard to adjust to some things. My life here as the wife of a shipping merchant, who is also new to the gentry is so opposed to my life at Holyfield and at the Queen's court. But I am far happier here with you, my love than I have ever been in my life."

Richard lifted her out of her chair and kissed her passionately.

Two months later after a particularly cold, wet spell of weather, the manor received an urgent message from Holyfield. Eleanor was very ill with a fever and cough. She had taken to her bed, which was most unlike her, and caused Edmund a great deal of alarm. Joan changed her clothes immediately, left a message for Richard to follow her, and headed for Holyfield on Caesar.

Upon Joan's arrival Edmund rushed her into the bedchamber. She found Eleanor wheezing badly, in between coughing fits. She was bathed in sweat and hot to the touch. Eleanor motioned Joan to bend closer to her. In between painful breaths, she indicated exactly what medication she needed and how it was to be prepared and administered.

Joan took off her cloak and made her way to the cupboard beside the kitchen where her mother-in-law kept her medicinal herbs and potions. She found the tincture of plantain leaf to relieve the fever and cough, the coriander for an infusion to reduce the fever, and finally the calendula syrup to ease the sore throat. When she was sure that she had all that Eleanor had asked for she returned to the bedchamber.

Joan dispensed a dose of each of the medications, taking careful note of when the next one was due. That done, she sent for a bowl of cooled, boiled water with which to bathe Eleanor's face and neck. Edmund had been watching the whole process in silence, his expression troubled.

He waited until he and Joan were alone downstairs before he asked her worriedly for confirmation that his beloved Eleanor would recover.

"I'm hopeful that she will, Father. Considering her age, she is very strong in body, and even more so mentally. She will fight this infection with every ounce of strength she has," Joan replied. "We will know more once the fever breaks. Hopefully her medication should begin to act soon."

Just after Joan had administered the second dose of medicine to Eleanor Richard arrived. He was shocked to see just how poorly his mother was. In all his life he had never known her to be ill, let alone confined to her bed. He looked from his mother to his wife, his expression reflecting his fear.

Joan reached for his hand. "We must give the medicine time to work and leave Eleanor to have some rest. Your father needs to rest, too. He's been up all night and is completely spent. I don't want to have two patients to nurse."

Richard went to sit in the parlour with Edmund, to keep him company until there was news, while Joan settled into the chair beside the bed. Eleanor fell into a fitful sleep and Joan continued to sponge her with the cool water as the fever raged and the coughing continued. After two hours of delirium Eleanor wakened and Joan repeated the medicine routine. Eleanor fell asleep again and Joan dozed on and off in the chair while checking her mother's condition regularly.

An hour before the dawn Eleanor's fever broke. The coughing continued but her breathing was a little easier; most of the pain in her chest was now muscular, on account of the coughing fits.

Joan managed to get Eleanor out of her bed and onto the chair. She then changed the bedding with the help of a maid before she dressed Eleanor in dry clothing. Soon Eleanor was back in bed. After yet more medicine she asked Joan to brush her hair. This is what Joan was doing when Edmund and Richard appeared just after dawn.

Edmund rushed to the bedside, tears of relief filling his eyes as he held his darling wife's hands. Richard looked first at his mother, who was propped up by her pillows, and then to Joan. He smiled at her in gratitude, only to notice how fatigued she was. "Mother seems so much better this morning, my love, but you look so tired," Richard said, and pecked her on the cheek.

"I feel very tired," she admitted, "and although Mother is improved, she is still a long way from being completely recovered. The medication is working and she is strong but we mustn't become complacent. She will need nursing for a while yet."

Eleanor suffered the nursing for three days before she insisted that she should be allowed to get up and sit in the parlour with everyone else. Edmund was pleased to see that her stubborn streak had returned, even if he wasn't sure that she was fit enough to be out of bed yet. But he knew that arguing with her would be futile and so she joined them in the parlour.

Two days later she declared herself well enough for Richard and Joan to return home. Richard knew that any contradiction would be useless and so after eliciting a promise from Edmund that he would send for them immediately at the first sign of any relapse, Joan and Richard left for the manor.

Good news was received by both Edmund and Richard shortly after Eleanor's recovery. Edmund had word via Adam's letter that his brother Gilbert, after weeks of exercises, was beginning to experience some feeling in his toes and was able to raise his right leg an inch or two. Adam said that Gilbert was keen to continue with the exercise regime even though progress was slow; at the beginning the physician had warned him that there may be no improvement at all, and that if there was it could take a long time to recover any kind of mobility. Nevertheless. Edmund was thrilled that there was at least hope of some improvement.

There had been a good harvest at Gilbert's farm too yielding more than enough food to keep the whole family fed for the entirety of the winter and early spring. His brothers' sheep farms were also doing well. Most of the ewes were expecting lambs imminently and there was also the prospect of first class fleeces this year. Edmund was delighted, as a good proportion of their flocks once belonged to him.

Richard had exciting news of another kind. Because Hubert had managed to procure a house for himself and his intended bride Katherine earlier than expected, their wedding had been brought forward to mid-summer. He hoped that Sir Richard and his wife, as well as Lord and Lady Lovell, would still be able to attend.

Hubert also informed Richard about an unexpected visit he had received at the office from an Oliver Dudley. Mr. Dudley operated a similar business to Richard between Hull and the continent. He was a middle-aged man who had made some handsome profits from his business over the years but had no family to hand his business on to. Mr. Dudley had decided that he would sell up and use the proceeds to enjoy what he hoped would be a long and happy retirement.

He had been in London to determine the cost of modest housing in one of the better areas, as he was hoping to make the city his home. He'd made tacit inquiries about shipping merchants who may be interested in expanding their fleet. In the process he heard of the success of Richard's trans-ocean fleet as well as the Topsham-to-the-continent side of his business. Mr. Dudley had called in on the off chance of speaking to the owner. Hubert had explained that he was only the clerk and that the owner was based in Devon. Dudley expressed his wish to speak with Richard about the prospect of doing business with him and confirmed would be willing to make himself available to Richard when he was next in London if that would be agreeable.

On the face of it Richard was interested. He would need to know a lot more, however, before he made any commitment, and he wanted to discuss it with his father first. Although Richard owned the business outright, his father had a wealth of experience as well as a keen business sense. Richard greatly valued his advice.

Joan accompanied Richard when he went to speak to his father at Holyfield. Eleanor and Edmund were sure that they would still be able to attend Hubert and Katherine's wedding, and so the ladies went off together to discuss clothes and wedding gifts, leaving Richard and Edmund free to go over the pros and cons of Mr. Dudley's offer.

It was decided that Edmund would make discreet enquiries, via some of his old shipping associates, about Mr Oliver Dudley of Hull. In the meantime, Richard would send a reply to Hubert agreeing to a meeting with the man while in London for Hubert's wedding.

Edmund's enquiries confirmed that Mr. Dudley's business was not only viable, but also hugely profitable. Ships, crews and clients were already in place and routes well established. Both Edmund and Richard deemed it a worthwhile investment if the price was fair. All that was left to work out was how much Richard could comfortably afford and how much his father was willing to let him borrow if the need arose. Hubert replied to Richard's letter, confirming that an appointment with Mr. Dudley had been arranged to take place in the London office.

When the time came to leave for London, Sam was excited; he'd never been outside Devon before. Agnes was less pleased to be making the journey next to him in the open air and acting as maid to Lady Eleanor as well as Lady Joan. Young Edmund was to remain at the manor with his nurse Mary.

The party reached London safely after a leisurely journey in mostly warm sunshine. Even Agnes found little to complain about. Once they had settled into their usual inn word was sent to Hubert and Katherine, inviting them to join the party for supper. Hubert was thrilled at the prospect but Katherine, who had only met Sir Richard briefly, was nervous. The poor girl had never met a lord and lady before, let alone eaten supper with them. When she was spoken to, she became tongue-tied and embarrassed. Joan's gentle manner soon put her at ease, however, and in no time they were all chatting together like old friends.

Katherine worked long hours in a local bakery. She began her day in the early hours assisting with the preparation and the baking before selling the bread on the street until late afternoon. She was a sweet, pretty girl and obviously as in love with Hubert as was he with her. Before the end of the evening Hubert had invited them all to visit his new home before the wedding. They settled on a day and time and agreed that the wedding gifts would be delivered then too.

When the Lovell family visited the house, they asked if Hubert and Katherine would allow them to arrange and pay for the breakfast feast. Hubert had been a godsend to Edmund's business when Richard had mysteriously gone missing from Topsham for weeks with no warning or explanation. He'd shown his worth again when Richard opened an office in London and Hubert had relocated there from Topsham. Since then, he had thrown himself into his work and had run the office and the warehouse almost single-handedly.

The day before the wedding Edmund and Eleanor attended an afternoon performance at the theatre, whereas Richard and Joan took a walk in the sunshine to the open courts to watch a game of tennis. They were enjoying their walk together, away from the hustle and bustle and the stench from the river, when they were confronted by a very unwelcome character coming from the opposite direction. He stopped directly in front of them.

Joan's heart missed a beat when she recognised Nicholas. She felt Richard tense beside her. Nicholas, on the other hand, seemed completely unperturbed by their reactions. Ignoring Richard he greeted Joan with a deep bow as he took her hand and kissed the back of it, never taking his eyes from hers.

Glaring at him, Richard growled, "What the

hell are you doing here?"

"Surely that's no way to greet a friend Richard," said Nicholas with a smile.

"You've never been a friend of mine!"

"Since you ask," Nicholas continued, as if he hadn't even heard Richard's reply, "my business is now almost entirely in London. Things are falling into place nicely and before too long we will be ready to act."

"We? I thought you were on our side now, you miserable turncoat!" Richard snapped.

"But, of course, Richard!" Nicholas replied, smirking. "However, when that time comes you will no longer be here to know for sure which side I'm on!"

Before Richard could react, the double agent continued at a brisk walk. Joan was horrified and Richard absolutely furious that Nicholas had dared to be so open with his threats in front of Joan. He was even more convinced that there would be further attempts on his life—and he knew all too well what would happen to his beautiful wife if the worst were to happen.

Hubert's was a quiet wedding with just a few guests: Katherine's parents, Hubert's father, Eleanor, Edmund. Richard and Joan. The bride wore a pretty blue dress which matched the colour of her clear blue eyes. She was adorned with a wreath of sweet-smelling herbs and flowers on her head and her dark brown hair hung down loosely onto her shoulders. Hubert was smartly dressed in his best clothes and looked on his lovely Katherine with eyes full of love and pride.

After the ceremony the group enjoyed the wedding breakfast at the inn, in a private room hired by Edmund. The tastiest of dishes were served with the best of wines and the meal was enjoyed by all. Just as she had put Katherine at ease on their first meeting so Joan did the same with the bride's parents, who also had never been in such company or partaken of such a rich meal.

Richard granted Hubert two days' leave after the wedding and Edmund handsomely compensated the baker to allow Katherine two days leave also. Richard informed Hubert that when he returned to the office, he would be promoted to head clerk with the relevant increase in salary and would have another clerk working under him plus two men in the warehouse. Hubert was delighted and relieved as he had been finding it difficult to cope with everything alone since the third ship joined the fleet.

Hubert had arranged the meeting between Richard and Mr.Dudley for the day after the wedding, when Richard would be managing the office until he returned from his short break. The man arrived on time, smartly dressed and with an air of confidence one would expect from a successful businessman. Richard greeted Mr. Dudley with a firm handshake and invited him to sit. The man insisted that Richard call him Oliver and they began their meeting with some general chit-chat about shipping in general before they got down to negotiations.

Richard had already worked out what he could pay for Oliver's business and how much his father would allow him to borrow should the need arise. The initial asking price Mr Dudley put forward was far higher than Richard could afford. When Richard protested, Oliver began to make case for how successful his business was.

"I have made it my business to discover for myself everything I need to know about your enterprise Oliver," Richard assured him. "I know how viable and successful it is, but the amount you are demanding is too high."

"I see you are astute and well prepared, Sir Richard. I am impressed by such business acumen in one so young," Oliver answered, but rejected Richard's counteroffer out of hand. He said that it would hardly cover the cost of the property he was planning to buy, leaving him next to nothing to live on.

The two men bartered backwards and forwards until they agreed on a deal which suited both. The price would be within Richard's price range without any borrowing, but Mr. Dudley had also insisted on a percentage of the profits from the business for the next five years. Richard managed to persuade the man to invest his dividends into his trading venture with America where good profits could be made every time the fleet returned. Both men were satisfied with the outcome and shook hands on the deal, promising to meet again in two days when all the relevant documents would be ready to be signed.

Pleased with his morning's work, Richard decided to go out for something to eat nearby before tackling the afternoon's paperwork. As he headed to the nearest tavern, he passed a young man on the dock who smiled nervously as Richard strode by. Upon Richard's return, the same man was pacing up and down the dock. Suspicious, Richard took a good look at him as he unlocked his office. Could he have been sent by Nicholas? He didn't look like an assassin, but then what did an assassin look like? Richard would make sure he was extra watchful when he left for the day just in case.

He hadn't been working at his desk for long when he heard the door quietly open and close. A shiver ran down his spine. Had the man decided to make his move now, while he was alone? Richard looked up, and nearly fell of his stool. Standing in front of his desk was Sir Francis Walsingham.

"Good afternoon, Richard," he said. "I hope I find you well."

Richard's heart dropped into his stomach. Why was this creature here? What suicidal scheme was he going to be blackmailed into this time? Surely the man wasn't stupid enough to disobey a direct order from the Queen?

"May I?" Walsingham asked. He gestured

toward the stool.

"Of course," Richard replied, trying to guess the purpose of the man's visit. Previously Richard had been summoned to Walsingham's office in the palace. Walsingham didn't come calling himself.

He settled himself, before he said, "Richard, I owe you an apology."

Richard couldn't believe his ears. He stared at Walsingham, as the spymaster continued, "I must assure you that I knew nothing about your arrest, your trial or your subsequent sentence. I was out of the country at the time."

"So I am led to believe," Richard returned. "However, when you were asked if you would have prevented it, your reply was not immediately forthcoming."

"Ah, I see you received a comprehensive report of my interview with Her Majesty. From John via Will perhaps?" Walsingham asked, raising an eyebrow.

"Does it matter?" countered Richard. "You would have let me die, an innocent man, sentenced to the most horrific of deaths."

Walsingham had the good grace not to defend himself. "Nevertheless, Richard, I do apologise."

"Do you, Sir Francis? Or are you just doing as you've been told by the Queen?" Richard demanded.

"No, Richard, I'm apologizing on my own behalf. I had no right to allow things to progress so far, for which I am truly sorry."

Richard looked into the man's eyes and was astounded to see actual remorse in them. "Very well, Walsingham. Apology accepted," he said, a little reluctantly. Changing the subject, he went on, "I suppose you know that Nicholas is here in London."

"Yes, of course, and he is being very closely watched."

"You don't trust the man, surely? You couldn't believe a word that comes out of his mouth!"

"I don't trust him an inch but he is still of some use to me," Walsingham said. "We are allowing him enough rope to hang himself, which he will surely do eventually."

"Are you sure that he is still working for you?" Richard asked.

"He is working for both sides, playing one against the other and enjoying every minute of it. What he doesn't seem to realise is that the information we feed him is mostly false with just an element of truth, whereas the intelligence we receive from him is mostly accurate. Don't worry about our friend Nicholas. He is heading towards a very sticky end."

"I see," said Richard slowly, hoping Nicholas's end would come before the man could order another attempt on his life.

Walsingham stood up to leave. "I'm afraid I must leave you now, Richard. Much to do, much to do."

He held out his hand. Richard shook it, and the

spymaster left as quietly as he had arrived.

Richard decided to close the office for the day as soon as could. As he turned to lock the door, he felt an unnerving sensation.

Someone was moving behind him.

Richard listened carefully, but it was difficult to hear anything over the thundering of his own heart. He had two options: flight or fight. He wasn't a man who ran away, but would he be able to draw his sword and turn quickly enough to strike first? As he moved his hand toward the hilt of his sword, still straining to hear any sound, a third party from another direction close by shouted out a warning.

Richard spun round. He caught the flash of the knife as his would-be killer also whirled in the direction of the voice—only for Richard's saviour to fell the cutthroat with a swift uppercut to the chin. The assassin dropped like a stone, the knife falling from his hand and landing at Richard's feet. Richard pushed his sword back into its sheath and picked up the murderer's blade. As he straightened, he saw the young man he had previously noticed on the dock standing beside the prone body. The young man was cradling his right fist in his left hand.

"I think I owe you my life, my young friend," Richard said, as he examined the killer's weapon. "Are you hurt?"

His rescuer grimaced. "I'm not sure, Sir Richard. I hit him harder than I'd intended. I'm

LIL NIVEN

hoping that I haven't broken my hand."

"Oh dear!" Richard took the lad's hand in his and examined it gently. "I don't think anything is broken, but it will be painful for a few days. That was some punch!" Richard glanced down at the man still sprawled at his feet, before he went on, "Now tell me who you are so that I can thank you properly. You seem to know who I am already."

"Ingleby! Roger Ingleby, Sir Richard."

He made to offer his hand to Richard before thinking better of it.

Richard laughed. "Very wise in the circumstances, I think," he said. "Pleased to meet you nevertheless, Roger Ingleby. Now we have been introduced you might tell me why you have been haunting the dock all day."

"I was trying to pluck up the courage to ask you for employment, but every time an opportunity presented itself I shied away," Roger admitted.

The would-be assassin began to stir. He seemed surprised to find himself on the ground. With some effort he managed to stand up. As he cast his eyes about for his knife, Richard drew his sword and held the point against the man's throat.

"Another failed attempt!" Richard commented angrily. "Your master is going to be less than pleased to discover that you were thwarted by a slip of a lad. Tell Nicholas that I have your blade and at the first opportunity I will bury it between his shoulders! Now take yourself off before I allow my blade to slip and slit *your* miserable throat!"

The man staggered down the dock and disappeared around the corner.

"Would you really have killed him?" Roger asked Richard.

"He wouldn't have been the first, nor probably the last," Richard answered resignedly. Dear God! When had he become so blasé about death? What kind of man was he becoming? "I am leaving for the day, but if you would care to come back tomorrow, perhaps we could discuss your request for employment further," he said to the young man.

"Yes, please, sir. I'll be here first thing!" Roger answered,

With a heavy heart Richard returned to the inn. When he explained what had happened to Joan, she burst into tears. "Oh, my love, how many more times before he succeeds? I can't go on like this much longer, forever afraid that something dreadful will happen to you, me or young Edmund. I'm tired of jumping at every sudden movement, of viewing everyone as a potential assassin. Some days I think I'm going insane!"

Richard put his arms around her and held her close. "That is all part of what he is trying to do, my poor darling," he said, "but we must not let him succeed with his mental torture. We must try to live our life as normally as we can, no matter how difficult that is. We will be returning home in a few days and leaving Nicholas behind."

Her mood lifted when he told her about his

successful business deal with Mr Dudley and his unexpected encounter with Walsingham.

"Do you think he really meant what he said when he apologised?" Joan asked him.

Richard shrugged. "With Walsingham, who knows?"

Roger was waiting for Richard at the office bright and early the following morning and explained how he'd come to know about Richard's business. It turned out Roger had been taught to fight by the same pugilist as Hubert, and the two had met at their lessons. Hubert had often spoke glowingly to him of his employer, Sir Richard Lovell.

Roger had been educated at a local grammar school and his parents had hoped that he would go on to university, but he wasn't interested in an academic career. Unfortunately, he had also failed to stick at any of the apprenticeships his father arranged for him. He had tried to explain to his father that he didn't want to work with his hands, but with his head; he enjoyed working with facts and figures. He could add and take away in his head quicker than Richard could do it with pen and paper. Unimpressed, his father had given him two weeks to find gainful employment. If Roger failed, his father threatened to disown him and leave him to fend for himself.

When Hubert mentioned that Richard would be attending the wedding and would be manning the office for a couple of days, Roger realized it was an ideal chance to ask about the prospect of employment. However, as Richard now already knew, Roger's courage had failed him at the crucial moment even though he had redeemed himself in a different way.

Richard explained that even though Roger had saved his life, as far as his shipping enterprise was concerned he was first and foremost a businessman who must have complete confidence that his employees were competent and reliable. He offered the lad a three-month trial with Hubert. If after that time he had convinced Hubert that he was capable of doing the job Richard would give Hubert permission to take him on permanently. Roger was delighted and promised Richard that he would complete all his duties diligently.

The following day Oliver Dudley arrived with the relevant paperwork to transfer his business to Richard. The contracts were signed by both men, witnessed by Richard's agent and Oliver's lawyer, and payment made. After bidding Oliver and his lawyer farewell, Richard stayed just long enough to wish Roger well in his new job and to thank Hubert for his part in making the family's stay in London so pleasant.

Richard went off to the inn with a spring in his step, whistling a tune to himself. At last preparations could be made for them all to begin the journey home. He was not a city lover and had missed his life at the manor, but not nearly as much as he'd missed his son.

# CHAPTER 13

Autumn was almost upon them when they arrived back at the manor. Young Edmund was delighted to have his mama and papa home again. Even though Joan and Richard had only been away for a few weeks they noticed a change in their son. He was not only walking confidently but seemed to prefer running everywhere now.

His vocabulary was also still expanding rapidly. He was quick to tell his parents that an 'enormous' disaster had occurred during their time in London. A wheel had come off his cart! Mary explained that Edmund had been trying to run too fast and had fallen. His cart had carried on down the hill until it hit a tree and came to a halt. Papa immediately demanded to know if the tree was still standing.

"Don't be silly, Papa! It was a BIG tree," Edmund chuckled, opening his little arms wide to demonstrate the point.

" What about your broken cart?" Joan asked.

"Oh, it's not broken now! Barnaby fixed it and I helped him," Edmund proudly told her. Then, after giving his parents a hug and quick kiss, Edmund decided that it was time to go outside to play with his cart.

"So much for us fretting that he would miss us," laughed Richard.

Joan had so enjoyed herself in London, visiting old friends and reacquainting herself with the sights, that Richard had half promised they would return for the Queen's Accession Day commemoration celebrations. Now that they were home again, however, he wasn't sure it would be possible. Accession Day was 17th of November, only two and a half months away. In that time he would need to go to Hull and make himself known to his employees, as well as meet and assess all his new crews and ships. Mr Dudley would have been in his office regularly but Richard would only be able to visit once or twice a year, so he had to assure himself that his people could run his business successfully without his permanent supervision—and more importantly, that they were trustworthy. He must do all this and get home to the manor in time to prepare for a trip to London.

Richard doubted this was possible. There were far too many uncertainties. Not wanting to disappoint Joan, he hadn't broached the subject with her before his parents arrived unexpectedly on their way to Topsham.

Eleanor went off to find Joan, while Edmund joined Richard in the parlour. He sat down besides the fire and warmed his hands. He watched his son pace up and down the floor for a few minutes before he spoke, "What's bothering you, son?"

Richard dropped into a chair by the fire and explained his predicament.

Edmund thought for a few moments before he remarked, "You seem to be on the horns of a dilemma. Do you go to Hull or do you go to London? Do you go to inspect your new acquisition and possibly not return home in time, thereby disappointing Joan dreadfully...or do you keep your promise and take her to the Capital and hope your business is sound? I can tell you from bitter experience it is not always wise to let your wife down!"

Edmund grimaced. Richard sighed.

"How much time do you have before you need to make your decision?" Edmund asked.

"Only two or three days. The more I think about it, the more convinced I am that I should go to Hull. I've just invested a great deal of money into the venture which I can't risk losing, but I hate the thought of telling Joan that we might not be able to go to London. She asks for so little and I know how much she is looking forward to the trip."

"Give me a little time to think about your problem," Edmund said. "I may be able to propose a solution, but I need to discuss it with your mother first."

By the time Eleanor and Joan eventually re-joined the men in the parlour, it was too late in the day to carry on to Topsham. Eleanor and Edmund decided to stay at the manor overnight and continue their journey the following day.

After breakfast the next morning, Edmund suddenly asked Richard if he was satisfied that Will was now capable enough to run the office single-handedly and would be able to cope alone with any problem that might arise.

"I think so, but why do you ask?" Richard returned.

"Since we received Adam's letter your mother and I have been talking about taking what would be our final trip to Yorkshire to visit your Uncle Gilbert and his family. We don't think we'll ever be fit enough to visit them again and so we thought we would make it a long holiday and stay over the winter."

"But, Father," Joan protested, "that's a very long way to travel and the weather will start to close in soon. Once the winter rain and snow arrive the roads quickly become impassable, especially for a coach. Are you sure you want to take that risk?"

"We have already written to Gilbert and if the reply is favourable, we could be leaving within days." Eleanor reassured her.

"Our only concern is whether you and Richard could manage the Yule celebration for the two estates," Edmund said, looking at Richard and then back at Joan.

"Of course we would be able to. After all, I've had the best of teachers all these years," laughed

Richard.

"I've also had a wonderful example to follow too, Mother," said Joan, smiling at Eleanor.

"That's settled then!" Edmund answered. "I can't see any reason why Gilbert and Sarah wouldn't welcome a visit and so we have been preparing for the journey for a few weeks now."

"I presume you were going to tell us you were going away for months before you actually left?" Joan asked somewhat humorously.

"Oh course, my dear!" Eleanor laughed. "After all, we will be leaving Holyfield and its staff in your care for the duration. Now can we go to the nursery for a while before we carry on to Topsham? I want to see my grandson, and Edmund wants to talk business with Richard."

Eleanor hooked her arm through Joan's and guided her to the door; on the way Joan looked towards Richard and raised her eyebrows before giving him one of her broad grins.

Once the door had closed Edmund said to him, "Now, son, as I am likely to be in Yorkshire for a while why don't you let me check over your business in Hull? I may have given the business over to you but I certainly haven't forgotten how a shipping company should be run!"

Smiling Richard answered, "Father, you can still teach me a thing or two about how to operate a business, I'm sure. I would be delighted if you could do that. Not only could you determine if the business is being run to its optimum, but you are also a shrewd judge of character. It would take you only a short time to discover if anything underhanded by the staff was involved and if my new employees were trustworthy and capable of carrying on unsupervised. As always, I would appreciate and value your assessment and advice on how to go forward, but are you sure it wouldn't be too much for you to manage? It is a considerable distance from Gilbert's farm to the port."

"That's enough of that!" snapped his father. "I'm already sick of your mother telling me that now I'm getting older I should slow down! I am not in my dotage nor will I be for some time yet! I'm sure Adam won't need much persuading to accompany me, either!"

"Of course, Father. I meant no offence," replied Richard, having been firmly put in his place.

"I look forward to getting into harness again, if only for a little while," Edmund confessed. "Sometimes your mother can be suffocating but with the best intentions in the world. I know it is only because she loves me, but at times I feel the need to escape for a while and this will give me the ideal opportunity."

"Very well, if you are sure, that would take a huge weight off my shoulders," Richard told him. "I really didn't want to let Joan down but couldn't see how to avoid it."

When the ladies returned Eleanor reminded Edmund that if they expected to be home before dark, they should leave for Topsham now. After they'd gone, Richard related his news to Joan, who was delighted to hear that now they would definitely be travelling to London. Richard was rewarded with a huge kiss and an enormous embrace which he gratefully accepted, the whole time wondering what her reaction would have been if he had told her they were unable to go!

Within the week his parents were on their way to Yorkshire, and Richard had taken on the responsibility of Holyfield's duties; both estates needed to be prepared for the coming winter before he and Joan left for London. Joan's excitement mounted the closer the day of their departure became. Richard, on the other hand, would have been much happier staying at home and not travelling for miles day after day in a coach. But a promise was a promise, and it filled him with joy to see Joan so exuberant.

Not everyone was happy that they were leaving. When he discovered that his parents were going away again without him Edmund threw a mammoth tantrum. Only the promise of a gift when they returned could assuage the little man's temper.

On the day of their departure Joan was sad to leave her little son behind, but as she kissed his chubby little cheek, she reminded herself that they would only be away for a few short weeks. The luggage was on board, Sam sat in his seat ready to go, Agnes waited inside the coach, and Caesar and Diablo were tethered behind it. Everyone said their goodbyes and Richard helped Joan up into the coach, before he settled himself into the seat beside her.

On wet days Richard and Joan remained inside the coach, but most days they rode their horses for at least part of the time. Neither of them liked being cooped up inside for long and relished being out in the fresh air. Agnes, on the other hand, complained about her back whenever the coach travelled over a particularly rough patch, until Richard demanded she stop unless she wanted to find herself sitting beside Sam.

They arrived in London three days before the festivities and booked into their usual inn, which was already nearly full of guests visiting London for the Accession Day Commemoration. After an early night Joan and Agnes spent the morning calling on Joan's old friends. Richard sent Sam along with them to deter any unwelcome attention and he went to his office.

Richard found Hubert and Roger busy at their desks. Hubert was delighted to see him and quickly confirmed that Roger was settling in nicely and was keen to learn all that was required of him. Richard was pleased to see how well the two men were getting along together.

Hubert then took Richard to the warehouse, which was mostly cleared; Richard's three ships were already well on their way to America on the last voyage for the year. However, the two new warehouse men were busy building extra shelving and racks to make the best use of the storage space. Richard was impressed and could visualise immediately what a tremendous difference their handiwork would make. Once again, he had been fortunate in his choice of employees.

When Joan and Richard met again at the inn later in the day Richard realised that she was in low spirits. Although she had thoroughly enjoyed visiting with her friends, it had hurt her more than she had anticipated that while they had been invited to the celebrations at the palace, she would never see the inside of the building again.

"I am sorry, my love, but we knew we wouldn't be going to the palace," Richard reminded her. "There will be many things going on in the streets, an abundance to see and hear as well as plenty to eat and drink. We will enjoy ourselves with Hubert and Katherine, I'm sure."

The next morning Joan put on a brave face as she and Richard, along with Agnes and Sam, walked through the streets. Hubert and Katherine would be joining them for the actual celebrations the following day as they both had to work until then. The Topsham party marvelled at the preparations. On the green they saw the archery butts being positioned for the coming competition, men digging pits for hog roastings, space roped off for the wrestling bouts, and stages being constructed for the musicians and players. Stallholders also were assembling their tables in anticipation of a good day's trade on the morrow. Bunting was strung between the houses, and depictions of the Tudor rose could be seen everywhere.

At the end of their excursion, they were all tired but excited. Agnes and Sam were delighted when Richard informed them that they could have the whole of the next day to themselves to enjoy the festivities.

Hubert and Katherine met Richard and Joan for breakfast at the inn in the morning and they all went off together to enjoy the celebrations. Joan wore a plain riding outfit, which was much more practical than one of her dresses, to wander the streets mingling with the general populace. Richard wore his sword and was pleased to see that Hubert had his as well; Joan's was wrapped up in the stable hayloft at home with the rest of her fencing gear, although she did carry a small dagger tucked into her belt.

There was so much to see it was hard to know where to go next. At the archery competition much money changed hands as folks bet on the outcomes. The wrestling was noisy and brutal; for the sake of the ladies, they didn't watch for long. Jugglers on stilts walked carefully through the crowds, delighting the children. Entertainment included puppet shows, music, singing and dancing, as well as plays performed on precarious stages hastily erected on the corners of the streets. Some stalls sold pies and pastries while others sold sweetmeats and cakes. Inns and taverns set up tables inside and outside for anyone needing refreshment while resting their aching feet.

All of London seemed to be out and about. Richard hoped his sword would deter any would-be pickpocket, but nevertheless he kept a tight grip on his purse, as did Hubert.

They were having a wonderful time—even Joan, who soon forgot her disappointment. As afternoon turned to evening, men lit bonfires and torches around all the greens, and the hog roasts were in full swing. Ale was dispensed from barrels placed all around the field. The music and dancing soon had everyone's feet tapping.

Both young couples joined in with the fun. Richard and Joan laughed and danced until they were completely out of breath, stopped for some refreshment and then did it all again. They hadn't felt so carefree for a long, long time. They barely noticed the group of soldiers pushing their way through the throng until the officer spoke to them.

"Good evening, Sir Richard," he said with a slight bow. "I must ask you and your companion to come with me immediately."

"How do you know who I am and how did you find me in the midst of all these people?" Richard asked, impatient to return to the dancing with his wife.

"I am well aware of who you and your wife are, sir." The soldier gave Joan a slight bow. "You have been followed discreetly since you left the inn after breakfast this morning. Now please, sir, if you will come with me."

"Why should we come with you?" Richard demanded. "We've done nothing wrong! We are just enjoying the celebrations!"

"I'm sorry, sir, but my orders are explicit. You are to come with me even if I have to arrest you both!"

"Both! What the hell has my wife got to do with this?" Richard stormed. As Joan moved closer to him and gripped his hand, he reached for the hilt of his sword with his other. "Arrested on what charge and by whose orders?"

The officer quickly covered Richard's hand with his. "You are not under arrest yet Sir Richard but If you refuse to come quietly, I have orders to shackle you. Don't make this difficult for both of us, sir."

"Richard, please don't do anything stupid," Joan pleaded. "I think we should go with him and sort this out with whoever sent him."

A horrible thought crossed Richard's mind as he looked at Joan's frightened face. Could these soldiers be Nicholas's men? Were they about to take him into a dark alley where he would be murdered and Joan kidnapped? It didn't bear thinking about but he knew he had no choice but to comply. "Very well," he said, "but I keep my sword!"

"Of course, sir. Now if you will follow me." Two soldiers went in front, pushing their way through the crowd, followed by the officer, Richard and

Joan, then two more soldiers at the rear. All the while Richard looked for any alleys leading off the street, but the soldiers showed no sign of deviating from their path. After what seemed an age of making their way through the press of humanity, they came to a halt at the palace gate.

Richard now knew exactly who was behind their abduction.

As he expected, the officer and two of the soldiers escorted Richard and Joan to Walsingham's office. Their escort was dismissed and Walsingham invited them both to sit.

"Not until you explain what the hell is going on!" Richard snapped. "Why were we lifted off the street like two criminals for no apparent reason?"

"You should know by now Richard that I do nothing without a valid reason." Walsingham said in his annoyingly calm, calculating voice. "Now please sit."

They sat down, feeling increasingly uneasy.

"Look, Walsingham, you've already been warned not to involve me in any of your scheming again," Richard reminded him. "Are you really willing to disobey your sovereign, despite the consequences?"

"You are correct, of course," Walsingham agreed, "but nothing was said about Joan."

He cast a furtive glance at her. Joan inhaled sharply.

Richard leapt up from his stool. "Oh no, Walsingham! You will not blackmail my wife into becoming part of one of your life and death intrigues! I forbid it!"

"You have no idea whose life or death is involved, Richard." Walsingham said, raising his voice.

"No, I don't, and I don't damn well care either! Joan and I are leaving now!"

When Richard took Joan's arm and began to guide her towards the door, Walsingham shouted "Sit down!" with such authority that Joan froze on the spot. Richard, however, turned and shot back, "No! We are leaving NOW!"

"Richard! If you insist on leaving I will have you tied down until you have both listened to what I have to say!" Sir Francis threatened.

"Richard, please," pleaded Joan. "Hopefully we'll be able to leave all the quicker if we do."

Grudgingly Richard released her and they both sat down again.

Walsingham cleared his throat nervously, which was out of character for the normally confident spymaster. "I have received reliable information that Nicholas is going to attempt to assassinate Her Majesty tonight," he said.

Joan let out a cry of dismay. Richard demanded to know why the man hadn't been arrested.

"I wish it was as easy as that, Richard. Most of those remaining in the palace overnight will be the worse for wear after excess eating and drinking at the Queen's celebrations and will be sound asleep in the early hours. Nicholas will enter the palace with an accomplice and neutralise the guards outside Her Majesty's apartments. Once Nicholas has entered the apartments the other man will leave and conceal himself outside underneath the Queen's bedchamber window to await the signal that will announce that our beloved monarch is dead. Only Nicholas and his associate will know what that signal is, as it won't be decided until they've entered the palace."

Walsingham paused before he continued, "The other traitor will then make his way out of the palace grounds and by way of a secret whistle will signify to the traitors waiting in the shadows that the deed has been done. This will begin a chain of events which will culminate in Spain's hoped-for uprising. Once it starts to gather momentum word will be sent to the Duke of Palma in the Netherlands, who will lead his troops across the Channel to claim England for King Philip of Spain."

"Good God can nothing be done to stop it?" asked Richard.

"Once the message reaches the rebels, we already have plans in place to arrest every last one of them before they can cause any mischief —but we can't do that until they rise against their country and commit treason! That means of course that we have to let Nicholas go through with his assassination attempt."

"Sir Francis, you are putting the Queen's life in jeopardy," Joan protested. "Does she know what is about to happen? What if it all goes wrong?"

"I have not informed Her Majesty as her reaction might imperil the whole enterprise. I think it best to leave her in ignorance. I need your skill, Joan. Nicholas is an expert swordsman —I don't know if he's ever been beaten. You are the best hope England has. You were taught by the greatest sword master in the land and you managed to even overcome him."

Richard jumped up again. "No, Walsingham, I absolutely forbid it!"

"I thought you realised by now that I will not be forbidden to do anything by you or anyone else," Joan snapped at him. Richard ignored her comment and carried on.

"I don't understand why Joan's life should be put at so much risk. You know the attempt on the Queen's life will be made tonight. Why can't you have soldiers lying in wait to arrest him as soon as he reaches her chamber?

"You must appreciate Richard that the success of this whole operation rests on the signal which will begin the uprising being given."

"Surely you have ways to force him to reveal the signal."

"We do but they wouldn't work in such a short time. I am hoping that when he thinks his opponent is a 'young boy' he will become over-confident and boast about the signal."

"And if he doesn't?"

"Then I'm afraid Joan will have to think of a way to tease it from him," Joan flashed

Walsingham a look of incredulity before Richard continued.

"Good God Walsingham is that the best you can do?"

"Until we know the signal we can do nothing. Everything rests on Joan's skill with the sword." Joan had been listening to the conversation between the two men intently. How had it come to this she thought in disbelief. I'm an ordinary wife and mother who wants nothing more than to be left in peace to live a normal life and yet now it appears I'm responsible for the survival the monarch and her entire realm.

"If Nicholas kills Joan what good would her knowing the signal be then?"

"If Joan dies so will the Queen and all will be lost!"

"My God man! You are standing by while two of the Queen's guards are murdered in cold blood and then expecting my wife to defeat a ruthless assassin like Nicholas!" shouted Richard." I will not allow it!"

"I'm sorry my love, but I don't think that's your decision to make," Joan said quietly. Richard was stunned.

"But you could be killed! Surely you wouldn't put your life at so much risk. What about me and young Edmund?" asked Richard, astonished that she could contemplate doing such a thing.

"Elizabeth is not only my sovereign but my friend," Joan reminded him. "I will not desert her or my country when they most need me."

"So much of a friend that she banished you from her sight as well as from the palace. She's not worth your life Joan," Richard said angrily.

"The law banned me, not Elizabeth!" she snapped. "Have you thought what will happen to our country if Nicholas succeeds? We would lose everything—possibly even our lives, including that of our son. England would be bathed in blood and those left at the end of it all would be forced to live under Spain's boot. I can't stand by and let that happen without at least trying to prevent it, my love." Joan gave Richard an imploring look. "Please try and understand. I love you so much it hurts, but if I don't do this you and all our people could lose everything they hold dear. Please Richard, I must at least try."

"But how can you fight when everything you need is in Devon?" Richard argued desperately.

Walsingham had remained silent during Richard and Joan's agonising dialogue. Now he spoke up. "I am sorry to disappoint you, Richard," he said, lifting something from behind his desk. "Once we knew of Nicholas's intention, I sent for this."

"If Barnaby has been hurt, I'll never forgive you," Joan shouted at him, as she recognised her own bundle from the hayloft.

"No-one was hurt, I can assure you. Barnaby was most co-operative, but he did send a message imploring you to take great care," said

Walsingham.

Joan took her things from Walsingham and turned towards Richard. She had tears in her eyes, but so did he. "Joan, please don't do this," he pleaded with her.

"I must, my love. If I don't succeed, England will never be safe again. I must at least try," she wept. "I don't want to leave you, but I must for all our sakes."

Richard turned toward Sir Francis. "If my wife dies, I will kill you!"

"If Joan is killed, I will surely be murdered myself soon afterwards. There is no way that Nicholas would allow me to live," Walsingham said in a matter-of-fact voice.

"You do realise that if Joan kills the assassin and the Queen discovers that you used her as bait, she will likely have your head anyway," Richard warned him.

"It's a chance I must take to keep her safe," Walsingham replied. "Joan, it is time. You must be in position before the traitor reaches the bedchamber."

As Joan and Walsingham moved towards the door, Richard made to follow.

"No, Richard," Sir Francis said. "Joan must do this alone. Wait here, I will return shortly."

Joan turned and almost threw her bundle at Sir Francis before she launched herself into Richard's arms. Richard gazed into her anguished face. They kissed each other passionately and clung onto each other until Walsingham once again reminded Joan that it was time to leave. Joan gently pushed herself away from Richard and left without a backward glance.

Sir Francis found an empty side room where Joan could change her clothes in private. When she emerged, she gave her riding clothes to Walsingham. She was wearing her sword and holding her hood and mask in her hand.

"Well, you certainly look the part," Walsingham said. "Let us hope that you can live up to your reputation."

Joan stared at the man coldly. "I can only promise to do my best. If that isn't good enough, I can do no more!"

"I meant no offence," Walsingham replied. "It's just that not only the fate of the Queen rests on your slender shoulders but also that of the whole nation. I will pray for your success!"

"As will I, Sir Francis."

When Walsingham opened the door Joan was relieved to see the corridor was lit by flaming torches placed at regular intervals. She had been afraid that she would have to feel her way to Elizabeth's bedchamber in the dark.

"The one vital piece of information we don't have is the time of the assassination attempt." Walsingham handed her a small stool. "Take this with you. It will make your wait more bearable."

Joan carried the stool with her as she left Walsingham and made her way to the bedchamber. Her mind flashed back to when she had been in the smuggler's cave, trying to find Richard lost in the myriad of tunnels. She was frightened then, and she was frightened now.

When she reached her destination, Joan made herself as comfortable as possible. She hoped her wait wouldn't be too long as she hated being confined in small spaces and was afraid her courage would desert her before Nicholas arrived. She thought of just how much her life had changed since she had met Richard. How they had instantly fallen in love at first sight, and the unexpected adventures they'd had together. How both had almost lost their lives, and the birth of her darling son Edmund. If she died, would he remember her?

Joan asked herself if she really believed could defeat Nicholas. If not, she was just throwing her life away. From nowhere she heard Lorenzo's voice. *Joan, pull yourself together! You are the best student I have ever had and I've taught hundreds. You must believe above everything else that you can defeat this man! Remember to always be alert to his dirty tricks and concentrate! You CAN do this!*

Joan was brought back to reality by a sound in the bedchamber The door where she hid was covered by a curtain; she opened it slightly to hear more clearly.

"Come now, you Protestant bitch, wake up and meet your nemesis!" Nicholas's voice bellowed.

"How dare you enter the Queen's bedchamber unannounced!" Elizabeth shouted startled out of her slumber. "Get out now!"

Joan heard the Queen's sleeping companion cry out as she jumped out of bed and scrambled underneath it.

"You can shout all you like but no-one is coming to your aid," Nicholas snarled. "You are going to die alone. Your death will mark the beginning of your miserable country's journey back to the Catholic fold where it belongs. Just as soon as I throw your stinking wig out of the window the revolution will begin. A heretic like you deserves no time to make her peace with God, but I will be generous and give you time—a very little time." Now she knew the secret Joan just had to kill Nicholas and give the signal, a task easier said than done.

Just as Nicholas stepped back a pace, Joan emerged from her hiding spot, and flung the stool at him. He deflected it just in time to meet her first thrust.

They parried backwards and forwards, tipping over tables and chairs and scattering Her Majesty's treasures all over the room. The initial sneer on the assassin's face soon turned to concern when he realised he faced an extremely skilled adversary. He jumped backwards over a small table as Joan's blade almost found its mark. She felt the pain just below her elbow when he retaliated and drew blood. Joan sliced the top of Nicholas's leg, causing him to shout out, but he came right back at her. She fell over the small stool cutting her left hand on some broken glass but rolled away and got to her feet before he could take advantage.

Joan forced him backwards until he almost landed on top of Elizabeth, who pummelled his face with her fists. As he spun away from the bed he picked up a book and threw it at Joan; she ducked out of the way. He came at her again. It was relentless. Lorenzo's voice spoke again. *Concentrate! You can do this, Joan! End it now!*

By now her arm was bleeding profusely as well as her hand, but she went at Nicholas with renewed vigour, her strokes almost as rapid as when she started. She pushed him back until he fell over a chair; Joan was on him before he had time to recover. She pierced his chest and he lay still. When she bent down to wipe the blood from her sword on his doublet, he opened his eyes.

"That perfume!" he gasped. "I know that scent."

She put her mouth to his ear and whispered, "Yes, you do. The great swordsman Nicholas Mortimer has been defeated by a mere woman. A woman who would have killed herself and her son before she would have surrendered herself to you! All your grand plans have come to nought."

With a look of pure disbelief on his face, he breathed his last.

Joan sheathed and sword, grabbed the Queen's wig from where it had fallen when its stand was knocked to the floor, threw it out of the window and ran for the secret door.

"Halt!!" shouted the voice of absolute authority. "I forbid you to leave until I know the name and see the face of my saviour!"

Joan turned slowly to face her dread sovereign as the terrified lady bed companion crawled out from under the bed to make her escape. When she opened the door to leave she nearly ran into Walsingham, who was about to enter with his soldiers behind him.

"You get out too!" the Queen shouted at him while picking up the nearest object which she hurled at her spymaster.

Walsingham retreated, smiling to himself. Not only had she survived, but Her Majesty's fiery temper was also intact.

Elizabeth turned toward Joan. "Now, boy, come here so that I can get a good look at you."

Joan obediently stood in front of her sovereign lady.

"Remove your mask and hood," the Queen commanded.

Joan did as she was bid. Her hair fell around her shoulders.

Elizabeth started. Her kind, loving and gentle lady-in-waiting stood before her as an avenging warrior, covered in blood. "Joan?" she exclaimed. "Is it really you?"

Joan dropped to her knees and bowed her head. "Yes, your highness. It is me."

"Up, up!" charged Elizabeth, and helped the exhausted heroine to her feet. "You saved my life by risking yours. I can never repay that kind of loyalty adequately."

Elizabeth put her arms around her champion and held her tight. When she released Joan again, Joan assured Elizabeth that no repayment was necessary. She already had everything she could possibly wish for in Richard and Edmund.

"Indeed, you are very fortunate, my dear friend, and I am sure Richard is desperate to know you are safe. Go to him now with my blessing." Elizabeth kissed Joan's cheek and whispered, "Thank you," before allowing Joan to leave. Just as Joan reached the secret door Elizabeth said, "Tell that oaf Walsingham that I will see him now!"

Joan struggled down the passageway, holding her wounded arm against her chest. Now that the adrenalin had stopped flowing, the pain had begun. When she opened the door at the end of the corridor she almost fell into Richard's arms; Walsingham had collected him after ensuring the Queen was safe, and the two of them were about to head up the secret corridor to meet her.

In a weak voice Joan told Walsingham that Her Majesty wished to see him and he obeyed instantly after informing Richard that he would send Dr Lopez to his office to treat Joan.

"My darling girl, you are hurt!" Richard exclaimed.

"I'm sorry, Richard," Joan managed. "I…"

Richard caught Joan as she fainted. Scooping her up in his arms, he hurried after Walsingham and entered the spymaster's office. Lopez was the man who had attended to Richard so diligently after he had been shot on his way back from France.

.Richard was sitting on a stool and cradling Joan on his lap when Lopez arrived.

The physician examined her arm. "That's quite a long gash but fortunately it's only a flesh wound. What happened to her hand?" he asked as he as he turned it over and wiped the blood from the lacerations.

"I've no idea!" Richard answered. "She passed out before she could tell me."

Lopez worked quickly to clean the wound on her arm before he stitched and bandaged it. He then made sure her hand was thoroughly clean before he put a dressing on it. Finally, he put her arm into the sling he had taken from his bag. "I suggest you keep her quiet for a few days," he told Richard. "She has been through a tremendous ordeal both physically and mentally. Her wounds should heal soon enough. She is an extremely fit young woman and a very remarkable one."

At just that moment Joan opened her eyes and groaned.

"It's all right, my sweet," Richard said softly. "You are safe now. It is all over."

"I want to go home," she whispered.

His timing perfect as usual, Walsingham returned to tell them that the Queen had ordered her own coach to be made available to convey

Richard and Joan to the inn.

"Can you walk if I help you?" Richard asked his exhausted wife.

"Yes, I'm sure I can." Joan slipped off his lap and stood up, albeit slightly unsteadily. They made their way to the outside door. Richard had his arm round Joan's waist to support her and helped her into the luxurious coach which awaited them.

Joan kept to her bed the following day. Agnes fussed over her, not understanding why her young mistress had been fighting again, or why the master had allowed her too. She began to wonder if Joan would ever settle down as a respectable married woman.

Richard had given Sam instructions to see that both coach and horses were ready to travel within two days. Richard himself had gone to speak to Hubert about their sudden disappearance the previous evening, without divulging any specific details. Although Hubert was curious, he knew it wasn't his place to interrogate his employer.

Joan and Richard had just finished breakfast on the day they intended to return home when a messenger arrived at the inn, looking for Joan. He bowed and handed her a small, embroidered pouch.

"Is there a message?" Joan asked, examining the little bag in her hand.

"No message, my lady. I was just told to deliver the package to you personally."

The messenger then bowed again and left.

"Well? Are you going to stand and stare at it all day or are you going to open it?" laughed Richard.

Joan untied the gold thread securing the top of the bag and tipped its contents into her hand. The ruby ring sitting in her palm made her gasp out loud. "Oh, Richard," she exhaled, "this is one of Her Majesty's favourite rings. She always wore it on her little finger. It must have meant a great deal to her, although why was never spoken about. And now she has gifted it to me!"

Richard smiled. "I believe it is to show you just how grateful she is. It is a beautiful gesture, but one you thoroughly deserve, my brave, brave darling. I am so terribly proud of you, even though I've never been so frightened in all my life, waiting to hear if you were alive or dead."

He took the ring and slipped it on Joan's slender little finger. It fitted perfectly. As she admired it, she said, "Whenever I look at this I will know that Elizabeth still loves me, despite what my misguided father and stupid brother did."

"How could anyone who knows you fail to love you, my sweet?" Richard answered. "But are you sure you are fit to travel? We could stay in London for a few more days until your arm has had time to begin to heal properly."

"No! I want to go home. I promise I will do as I'm told—at least until my arm is healed," she purred, flashing Richard one of her special smiles.

"You are nothing but a naughty minx! I do not

believe you've ever done as you were told in your life! Maybe that is why I love you so much!" Richard said and kissed the end of her nose. "Come on, then. We'd better get started."

During the trip Joan and Richard decided that since little Edmund had reached the age of four years they would try to purchase a pony for him on the way home. The previous year the breeder in Exeter had nothing suitable and so they were delighted to find he now had a good stock of young animals ready for the saddle. Richard picked out a well-behaved white pony and bought the relevant tack to go with it.

It was already getting dark when they reached the manor. The two horses and the pony were left with Barnaby at the stables, while the coach carried on to the house. Henry met them at the door; he raised an eyebrow at Joan's sling but said nothing.

Edmund had heard his parents' voices and despite Mary's protestations came bounding into the parlour from the nursery .He stopped in his tracks when he saw his Mama's injured arm but was quickly assured that Joan had had a little accident but all was now well. After much hugging and kissing Richard announced that they had forgotten something and needed to go back to the stables.

"Is Sam home? Can I come, Papa? Pleeeease?" Edmund begged, so the three of them went off hand in hand to the stable. As soon as he saw Sam,

Edmund rushed towards him with his arms open; Sam swung him round and round, much to the child's delight.

When Sam put him down again Richard beckoned his son towards the usually empty stall, where the pony was. Edmund's eyes nearly popped out of his head.

"Is that a big enough present?" asked Richard, laughing at the expression on his son's face.

"Is he really mine, Papa?" Edmund exclaimed, his eyes darting between his parents.

"He is as long as you look after him properly and do as you are told when you ride him— and that's not just from me and Mama, but from Barnaby too," Richard warned him.

"I will, Papa, I promise. What is he called?" Edmund asked Joan.

Smiling, Joan replied, "I've no idea because you haven't told me what you've named him yet."

Richard picked his son up and put him on his shoulders. "You can think about that in your dreams. If Mary tells us in the morning that you have been the very best of boys, we'll put his little saddle on and we'll see how you cope up on his back. Now it's bedtime!"

The next day Barnaby led the pony with Edmund on his back round and round the yard. Richard walked beside his son, keeping him steady in the saddle just as his father had done with him all those years ago. He hoped that Edmund would cherish the memory of his first time in the saddle as much as he did. Edmund didn't want to stop but cheered up when Richard told him that now he would learn how to groom his mount with Barnaby's help.

Joan and Richard had spent a considerable time persuading Edmund that 'Sam' perhaps wasn't the most appropriate name for his pony. It was only after Joan had pointed out that the little creature was completely white without a single mark on him that Edmund proudly announced his name had to be Snowflake.

In the run up to the Yule celebrations Richard and Joan worked hard on the preparations, making sure that nothing was overlooked and that all was in place for the celebrations at Holyfield Hall. There had been some snow but on the day of the festivities it was bitterly cold; Richard lit extra braziers to keep the villagers warm for their feast. No-one seemed to notice the chill during the feast, and when they had finished at the tables the children kept warm chasing each other and playing games.

By the time the festivities ended the temperature had plummeted, prompting Richard to arrange for Barnaby and Sam to take two wagons for the children and those not capable of walking back to the villages. It was dark and even colder by the time the two men returned with the wagons. Richard met them at the stable with a good tot of his precious brandy, plus a plate full of pies.

Richard, Joan, young Edmund and their staff returned to the manor three days later to discover that Will had already returned from spending the Yule with his father in Exeter. During a stopover at The Bush on his way to the manor the landlord had handed him a package for Richard.

"It will be from Tom Ashe," Richard said, taking the package from Will. "With all that has been going on I hadn't realised we were still to hear about the ships' return to America."

Richard opened the package and gave Joan her usual letter from her mother before he opened his own correspondence. He was delighted to hear that the wharf was nearing completion and would be ready by the spring. Business was booming at the store but it was in dire need of more storage space. Perhaps a small warehouse, Tom suggested. More homes were being built as new colonists arrived, including a physician, a blacksmith, a couple of farmers with their families and skilled tradesmen. The outlook was positive.

There was some concerning news, however. Thomas rarely left his chair now and found walking difficult. The new physician had examined him and confirmed that Thomas wasn't suffering from sickness or disease but advancing age; he feared Joan's father would not see out another year. Tom was of a mind that Richard's business in the colonies needed his personal attention, and soon, if things were to carry on smoothly. He wondered if Richard would be able to return with his ships on their next voyage.

This was unexpected, but Richard knew that Tom was right. He had to find replacements for Thomas and Margaret and ensure that his business interests there were safe. He didn't relish the thought of leaving Joan and Edmund for months and knew that Joan would object. He glanced over at her, wondering how he could break the news gently, and noticed the tears falling.

"My father is dying, Richard," she wept.

He put his hand on her shoulder. "I know, my darling; Tom told me in his letter. I am so sorry." Richard paused before he continued, "Tom has suggested that I go to America myself when the ships return in the spring. I don't think I have a choice, Joan. There is much to do to ensure that the business continues to thrive. I won't be away for any longer than necessary."

"I agree. We won't take any longer than we need to."

"We?" Richard repeated, alarmed by Joan's implication. "Oh no! I will be going alone! It is the nearly the other side of the world! Anything could happen!"

"If or when it does, we will face it together. We are a family, Richard, and Edmund and I will not be separated from you for months on end."

"But Edmund is only four years old! The answer is no!" Richard insisted.

"Have you any idea how long a month is to

a four-year-old?" Joan retorted. "I do not intend my father to die without having met his only grandchild. We are all going together and there's an end to it. Don't you dare say you forbid it because I'm not listening!"

Richard stared at her, horrified. But at the same time, he knew that however much he opposed the idea, once his wife had made up her mind the devil himself couldn't change it. They would all be going to America.

# THE END

# ABOUT THE AUTHOR

## Lil Niven

Lil lives in the small Ayrshire town of Mauchline in Scotland with her husband Pete. She is the mother of three grown up children, Loraine, Elizabeth and Heather and grandmother to Aidan. She enjoys walking, gardening, reading and crafting when not writing books. This is the third of four books in this series.

Printed in Great Britain
by Amazon

21742954R00165